Tiffin &
TRAGEDY

A Tea & Sympathy Mystery

BOOK 3

J. NEW

Tiffin & Tragedy
A Tea & Sympathy Mystery
Book 3

Copyright © J. New 2021

The right of J. New to be identified as the author of this work has been asserted in accordance with the Copyright, Designs and Patents Act 1988. All rights reserved. No part of this publication may be reproduced, stored in or transmitted into any retrieval system, in any form, or by any means (electronic, mechanical, photocopying, recording or otherwise) without the prior written permission of the publisher. Any person who does any unauthorised act in relation to this publication may be liable to criminal prosecution and civil claims for damages.

This is a work of fiction. Names, characters, businesses, places, events and incidents are either the products of the author's imagination or used in a fictitious manner. Any resemblance to actual persons, living or dead, or actual events is purely coincidental.

Cover design: J. New.
Interior formatting: Alt 19 Creative

OTHER BOOKS BY J. NEW

The Yellow Cottage Vintage Mysteries in order:
The Yellow Cottage Mystery (Free)
An Accidental Murder
The Curse of Arundel Hall
A Clerical Error
The Riviera Affair
A Double Life

The Finch & Fischer Mysteries in order:
Decked in the Hall
Death at the Duck Pond
Battered to Death

Tea & Sympathy Mysteries in order:
Tea & Sympathy
A Deadly Solution
Tiffin & Tragedy

Chapter One

*S*UMMER WAS NOW in full swing in the small town of Plumpton Mallet, and Lillian Tweed was busying herself at her Tea Emporium with a sudden though very welcome intrusion of a town tour group. Usually when the coach holiday company brought day trippers through, it was a relatively small crowd containing only two or three people actively looking to purchase. Today, however, the group was full of Americans who all wanted an authentic British tea set and various selections of teas to take home from their European holiday, and it was an absolute madhouse.

Lilly and her shop assistant, a young college student named Stacey who also happened to be from the states, were doing their best to ensure each of the nearly thirty customers were being taken care of. From explaining the history of tea, to brewing numerous samples and explaining their health benefits. From demonstrating how to set the perfect tea table to acquainting them with the manufacturers and artists who designed and hand painted the china. Lilly was determined that each and every customer received the full experience and left her shop happy and full of additional knowledge. Earl Grey, former stray and now official shop cat, had bolted for the back room to hide from the crowd almost as soon as they'd made an appearance.

This exposure was something fairly new and Lilly was still getting used to it. Her business had been open for less than a year, but the coach company had only added her shop to the stopover in the past spring. So far, the groups had been small compared to what they were now getting during the summer months.

Several of these first-time customers wanted their orders shipped back home to the states while others were trying to choose something that would be a bit more durable and safer to take on board the aircraft. Lilly and Stacey did their best to help them pick out something for their specific needs and taste, since most of the group did not appear to be regular tea drinkers. It was more being able to return home and show off their quintessential British collectables, Lilly supposed, but if it was also about introducing a bit of additional knowledge and culture to the group as well as making a good sale in the process, she was more than happy to go the extra length.

A total of sixteen complete tea sets were purchased by the time the group was ready to move on, along with a number of collectable tea cups and saucers, six teapots and numerous sundry items such as the hand embroidered tablecloths and napkins. The tour guide, who had become a familiar face over the previous months, gave Lilly a thumbs up as he shuffled his group out of the door. He knew this had been the most profitable crowd to have come through so far. He was still grinning at Lilly and Stacey through the large front window as the last of his tour goers trickled out of the shop to catch up with him.

"Whoa," Stacey said, collapsing on one of the bar style stools that lined the front of the main counter. She looked dizzy and a bit shell-shocked from the whirlwind that had just gone through. The shop had occasional bursts of customers, but nothing like what they had just experienced. Usually it was half a dozen or so at a time and half would be merely browsers.

"You're telling me," Lilly said, laughing and taking a seat herself. "I don't think the shop has ever had as many customers at the same time. All requiring attention considering they had very little knowledge about teas and teapots. You did a brilliant job of keeping your head and not getting flustered or overwhelmed. Well done, Stacey."

"After that, I see what you mean by my fellow countryman's abrasive personality," Stacey said, laughing at herself as much as the recent customers. "I've got so used to dealing with the locals, I'd almost forgotten how loud we Americans can be. Gosh, am I really that loud, Lilly?"

Lilly laughed. "I've never once said you're abrasive. And no, you're not that bad, Stacey."

"I feel like you wanted to add *anymore* to the end of that sentence."

Lilly chose to remain quiet, neither confirming nor denying Stacey's statement. It was true when Lilly had first met the young woman, she had nearly burst her ear drum with her constant peppy chatter. Stacey had marched into the shop almost demanding a job, partly for the same reason the American crowd had just bought half her merchandise, hoping for a truly British experience. But also to help with her college education and rent. Since then, though, Stacey had become as much of a tea drinker as the average Plumpton Mallet resident. Not to mention exceptionally knowledgeable about the teas. She was a godsend to Lilly and her business. And now that she was living in the flat above the shop for a much reduced cost, she was also on hand whenever Lilly needed her.

"After a crowd like that, I admit to having second thoughts about whether I should go tomorrow," Lilly said, thinking of a celebration she'd been invited to. She'd been hesitant all week about leaving the shop for the weekend trip, and after the crowd they'd just dealt with, her hesitancy had only grown. It was summer, and the number of customers would only increase.

"Lilly, come on," Stacey groaned, clearly having grown a bit fed up of the agonising back-and-forth Lilly had been experiencing all week. "You've been talking about how much you're looking forward to seeing your friends Robert and Joanne for almost a month now. Don't you go getting cold feet just because we had one day that was a little busier than usual. I seriously doubt we'd get another crowd in like that while you're away for just a few days, and even if we did, I could totally handle it."

Lilly smiled at her young assistant. It was true she was very much looking forward to the visit. "I know," she said. "And I also know you're more than capable of dealing with whatever is thrown at you. That crowd was just a lot to handle, that's all."

Earl Grey came meandering out of the back room, obviously having sensed the large crowd had finally dispersed. He effortlessly jumped up onto the main counter where they were both sitting, enjoying a well earned cup of tea. It was the remains of one of the sample pots brewed for the tourists, and neither one wanted to see it go to waste.

"And besides," Stacey continued, reaching out and scratching Earl behind his damaged ear, his favourite spot, "Earl Grey will be here to help me hold down the fort. Won't you, buddy?"

Lilly laughed and rolled her eyes. "Oh, well, that completely puts my mind at rest. I appreciate you being so willing to look after the shop and Earl during my absence. Though I don't know how much help he'll be if he runs away and hides, like he did today. It will be really nice to see Robert and Joanne again, it's been ages since we were together. I don't think I've seen them in person since their wedding, and that was five years ago. We've just talked on the phone or sent the occasional email or card for birthdays and Christmas. They haven't managed to get back to Plumpton Mallet since they got married and I know I haven't been anywhere."

"Wow, five years is a really long time without a break, Lilly. You can't work all the time, it's not good for you," Stacey said. "So, how do you know these people exactly?"

"It was from my Agony Aunt days," she replied, giving their cups a refill.

Prior to opening her shop, Lilly had been the advice columnist for the Plumpton Mallet Gazette. The paper had been taken over by a larger concern and as they already had an Agony Aunt on staff, she was made redundant. Her redundancy money made up part of what she had used to open her business. She'd written a lot of advice columns in the days leading up to the takeover.

"Oh? Did they work at the paper as well?"

"No, actually, Robert wrote a letter in to the paper," Lilly explained, thinking back to the occasion with fondness. "It was anonymous, which is par for the course with an advice column, so obviously I didn't know who had written it at first. He needed some advice about a woman he was interested in, a divorcee, because he'd been out of the dating game for so long. He was a widower and a single father. He didn't know the best way to approach it without making a mess of things, or appearing too keen and desperate, so I helped him. A few months later, they both turned up at the paper to thank me and show off the engagement ring. We've been friends ever since. I was invited to their wedding which was beautiful, they have great taste. I think that's the last time I saw them face to face, though. I got to know them both well during their engagement period and ended up helping with some of the wedding preparations."

"That's so sweet, and so romantic. It was you that got them together," Stacey said approvingly. Earl had now moved from the counter to her lap, and she was continuing to stroke his back while they chatted above the audible purring.

Lilly nodded, smiling. "That's what they both say, although I'm sure Robert would have worked it out on his own, eventually. Now they have a bed-and-breakfast on the coast down south and are celebrating their five year wedding anniversary. It's a family occasion, so I was a bit surprised to get an invitation, although I think Joanne wants some help with the planning and decoration, and my teas."

"No surprise, as far as I'm concerned. They probably think of you as family. Besides, you do make a great cup of tea."

THE BELL ABOVE the shop door chimed, so Stacey stood up and Earl hopped down to the floor, giving a languorous stretch of each individual leg before making his way to his favourite spot in the window, where he curled up and went to sleep. Lilly turned and smiled.

"Archie," she said, happy to see her old friend Archie Brown paying a visit.

"Good afternoon, ladies," he said, tipping his old-fashioned hat. "I understand my teacup is ready?"

"It is indeed," Lilly said. She was particularly proud of this repair. It had been in a sorry state when Archie had first brought it to her and had taken much longer than she'd expected due to its delicate nature. "Stacey, would you bring it through?"

"Sure will," she said, disappearing into the back room while Lilly stepped back behind the counter and Archie took the bar stool she had just vacated.

"So, how have you been, Archie?"

"A lot better, actually. Ever since Douglas had a personality transplant and started calming down. She must have visited Stepford recently."

Lilly laughed. Abigail Douglas was the new Agony Aunt at the paper and had been banging heads with Archie since day one. Archie was the senior crime reporter at the gazette, a position Abigail had set her sights on once she realised her column was all but dead, and was quite vocal about how much he missed Lilly at work, particularly considering the type of personality who'd taken over her job.

"You two are getting on better, then?"

"As well as can be expected, I suppose," he said. "She even asked me to pass on her regards to you. Can you believe that? I suppose she's having to adjust her attitude considering the results from your last case."

"Case? Good grief, Archie, you're making me sound like detective."

"You're two for two, my friend," Archie responded, referring to the hot water she'd managed to get herself into over the previous few months. On two separate occasions Lilly had managed to solve a local murder and earned herself a bit of fame in the process. The gazette had even done a couple of stories about her, deeming it front-page headline news both times. The first article had been co-written by Archie and Abigail, on the second Archie had taken the reins himself, which was how it should be. Lilly had enjoyed being interviewed by her old friend, especially as the articles had meant a spotlight had been shone on her business to positive effect.

"She's not still upset about my Agony Aunt letterbox, is she?" Lilly asked, referring to the one she had had fitted at the shop for people to continue to drop off advice requests. It hadn't been intentional to continue giving personal guidance once she'd left the paper, but people had reverted to contacting her at the shop, much to Abigail's chagrin. She'd feared the paper would nix her column completely if people didn't start writing in, causing her to lose her job. It was a fear Lilly admitted had some merit. But she couldn't stop people writing to her, nor could she ignore their requests for help.

"She hasn't mentioned it in a while, actually," Archie said. "So we'll see. I'm hoping she'll continue on this pleasant path at work. She's starting to get along with several other members of staff now she's stopped harassing and bad-mouthing you. You're still popular among the staff at the paper so her antagonism toward you wasn't doing her any favours. Quite the opposite, in fact. At least she's seen reason now, thank goodness."

Stacey arrived back, holding a small box that she gingerly placed on the counter between Lilly and Archie. Lilly grinned and opened the package, carefully lifting out the contents, and placed it before Archie for him to examine.

"So, what do you think?" Lilly asked, as he picked up the teacup with a grin as big as the one Lilly was wearing.

"Absolutely incredible," he said. "I'd just about destroyed this poor cup. I honestly didn't think you'd be able to repair it at all, Lilly. Now look at it. It's like magic. You can't even see where it was damaged. I have no idea how you managed to do it, but I really am very impressed, my friend. The real question is whether it will do its job. Will it hold my tea?"

Lilly smiled. "Only one way to find out, Archie. Let's test it. I have some mint tea already brewed, how about that?"

"Perfect, I love mint tea. Do the honours, would you?" He said, placing the cup on its saucer and sliding it towards Lilly.

She swilled it out, then poured the tea. As she expected, and much to Archie's delight, it worked perfectly. For much of the afternoon, in between spells of serving customers and taking in deliveries, the three of them laughed and swapped stories before Archie realised how much time he'd let sneak by. He once again thanked her profusely for the repair as he departed, and before Lilly knew it, the day was over.

It felt very strange leaving Earl behind with Stacey, who lived in the flat above the shop, but she had to go home and pack ready for her early morning start. She had a long day of driving ahead of her tomorrow. She rode her bicycle home to her little cottage on the outskirts of town and realised how much she was looking forward to a rest and a fun weekend with her friends.

Unfortunately, the celebrations wouldn't go according to plan and if she'd known what was about to happen, she would never have gone.

Chapter Two

ALMOST SIX HOURS after she had set off from home, Lilly finally joined the winding back road that would lead her to the bed-and-breakfast. She'd never had the opportunity to visit before, but Joanne had sent her pictures, and she thought she had a rough idea of what the place was going to look like. However, nothing had prepared her for the extravagance of the building and its striking setting. The photos really hadn't done it justice.

The bed-and-breakfast was located on England's southern coast, perched on a coastal cliff with a panoramic view of the sea. As she stepped out of the car, stretching her back to get the kinks out after the long drive, she could taste the tang of salt in the air and smell the warm sand and the kelp. The balmy weather was perfect and she could already envisage daily trips down the private steps to visit the beach below the cliff.

"Wow," Lilly breathed softly, trying to take it all in.

She glanced back the way she had come. The long drive was as picturesque as all the other parts of the property she could see from where she stood. Numerous trees, probably older than she was, grew majestically alongside a smaller, more recently planted orchard, filled with apple trees and other assorted specimens she couldn't name. The more formal gardens, which she could see from where she had parked, were accessed via an ornate white archway leading to a little path flanked by large, colourfully flowering shrubs. Rhododendron and Hydrangea she thought. As well as several Palm trees which gave the bed-and-breakfast its name.

The property itself was of a moderate size. Her friends had told her it hosted ten separate guest suites along with a private lounge and bedrooms for the owners, and smaller suites for the live-in staff. It was an older house built in the late eighteen hundreds in a timeless Art Deco style and painted an opaque white. It looked incredible against the deep blue of the summer sky. *It almost glows,* Lilly thought as her friend came rushing down the steps, arms outstretched, to welcome her.

"Lilly!" she exclaimed, her long sun dress flowed behind her as she ran, and a sneaky breeze nearly whipped the large beach hat from her head.

She looks incredible, Lilly thought. The last five years had obviously been good to her friend.

"Joanne, gosh it seems like forever since I last saw you."

Joanne threw her arms round Lilly in dramatic fashion, laughing like a school girl.

Tiffin & Tragedy

"Lilly, I am so glad you're here. Thank you for coming, it's going to be great to catch up this weekend. And you must tell me all about your tea shop."

"Try to stop me," Lilly said with a smile. "This place is absolutely amazing, Joanne. You and Robert must have worked so hard to get it looking this beautiful. The pictures you sent must have been when you first took over?"

"Yes, we've painted the whole place inside and out since then, as you can see," she said with a broad sweep of her arm. "It gave the place a much needed face lift. Come on, let me help you with your bags and get you settled in your room, then I'll give you the grand tour. So, how was the drive?"

"Long. Six hours," Lilly said with a slight groan. "Although I did stop for lunch."

"You really should have caught the train, you know. Robert would have picked you up at the station. You could have been here two hours ago."

"I know, but I had too much luggage. I've brought a full tea set with me. One of my best."

"You didn't have to do that," Joanne exclaimed. "We've got perfectly good sets here. I just wanted you to bring along some of your speciality teas. We have nothing like your shop down here."

"Well, I did that too, but the set is an anniversary present for you both," Lilly explained, opening the boot of her car.

"Lilly, that's so kind of you. You really didn't need to bring us anything, you're already coming early to help us get ready for the party."

"I wouldn't dream of coming empty handed, Joanne. Besides, I wanted to get you something special."

Lilly pulled her suitcase out.

"Here, let me get that," Joanne insisted, taking the case from Lilly's hand. "Now, let me show you to your room."

⁂

THEY ENTERED THE bed-and-breakfast through the main front door, and Lilly gazed up at the crystal chandelier that was causing a dazzling light display, thanks to the influx of sunlight from one of the higher windows.

"That's absolutely stunning," Lilly said. "It's like being in the foyer of a fabulous cruise ship from a hundred years ago."

"I know, I love it. Although it's a bit of a dust gatherer. We have to clean each individual glass droplet every six months, otherwise it loses its shine. It's worth it though."

A woman in a beige calf length shirt dress and matching espadrilles came hurrying to the door when she heard it open.

"Welcome to The Palms," she said in a soft and quite sultry voice.

"Natalie," Joanne said. "This is my very good friend Lilly Tweed. She's going to be staying with us for a few days and has generously offered to help with the party. Lilly, this is Miss Natalie Sampson, our housekeeper. And a very good one at that."

Natalie put out her hand. "Nice to meet you, Lilly. Joanne has been telling me about your shop. You're the person to go to when it comes to tea, apparently. We provide Tiffin for the guests every afternoon at three o'clock, so I would love to pick your brains at some point, if I may?"

"A pleasure to meet you, too. And yes, of course, I'd be happy to help," Lilly said.

Miss Sampson escorted both ladies upstairs and along the hall to one of the suites. Lilly was delighted to find her room had a glorious view of the sea and the private beach.

"Oh, this is absolutely beautiful. What a gorgeous place to live," she said, gazing out of the window as Natalie Sampson carefully placed Lilly's bag by the door.

"I'll just go and get you your room key," Natalie said before disappearing.

"I don't know what I'd do without Natalie," Joanne said to Lilly. "She runs the place like clockwork."

"So, where's Robert?" Lilly asked, gazing around the beautiful room she'd been given. It was a timeless luxury in an Art Deco style, with much of the features obviously original. An antique double bed with matching wardrobe and dressing table were the main pieces of furniture. But in the bay window sat an occasional table with two club chairs in teal velvet. She was really going to enjoy staying here.

"He and Chloe went to have a father daughter early dinner in town," Joanne replied, already half way out of the door, eager to show Lilly around the place.

"Gosh, I haven't seen Chloe since your wedding. How old is she now?"

Lilly had never got to know Chloe very well. She'd been quite young and very shy when she'd first met Robert.

"Sixteen. Can you believe it? And let me tell you, she has really come out of her shell."

"I bet you had a lot to do with that. How do you like being a step mum?"

"I honestly love it, Lilly. Admittedly Chloe makes it very easy, she's such a sweetheart."

Lilly smiled as she followed Joanne down the hallway, where her host showed off a number of the rooms, each with their own unique and stunning design. She opened up the final door leading to one of the larger guest suites and almost crashed into a young man.

"Oh," she yelped.

"Sorry, Aunt Joanne," he said. "I was just putting new sheets on the bed."

"No, that was completely my fault, Dominic. I should have knocked before charging in like a bull. Lilly, this is my nephew Dominic, he works with us, too."

"Looks like it's a family affair around here," Lilly said. "Nice to meet you, Dominic. Do you like working at The Palms?"

"Absolutely," he said with a pleasant smile.

Dominic was quite young, in his mid twenties, Lilly thought, but she got the impression he was a dedicated employee and more mature and serious than a lot of his contemporaries.

"How long have you worked here?"

"A couple of years now. My brother Edward and me got summer jobs after we'd finished school, but I stuck it out a little longer than him. You'll get to meet him, though. He and mum are coming to help Aunt Joanne and Robert celebrate their anniversary. We're all really happy for them, he's a really nice guy. You're the one he wrote to asking for dating advice, is that right?"

Lilly laughed. "Yes, that's me. But how on earth did you know?"

"Are you kidding? Aunt Joanne's been staring out of the window for the past hour waiting for you to arrive," he said, earning him a playful thump on the arm from his aunt. "Hey, I'm just saying you're really excited to have your friend here. She showed me the articles about you in the Plumpton Mallet Gazette."

"Really? Wait, surely you don't get the gazette all the way out here? Their circulation isn't that big, unless it's changed a lot since I left."

Joanne shook her head. "No, we have a subscription. They send it on to us by post. Plumpton Mallet is our home town, so it's lovely catching up and seeing what everyone is up to. Especially when it's one of my closest friends. Besides, we have a bit of a soft spot for the paper because it was your agony aunt column and advice that brought us together."

"Oh, by the way, Aunt Joanne, did Natalie tell you about the little mishap?"

Joanne raised an eyebrow. "What mishap?"

Dominic sighed. "I don't know whose error it was, but one of the rooms has been booked for a guest this weekend."

"What? Oh, no. I thought we blocked this weekend off for friends and family with no overnight guests apart from Lilly so we could have the party?"

"I'm sorry. I don't know how it happened, but the guy is already here. I showed him to a guest room. I wasn't sure what to do, but I didn't think it was right to turn him away, considering he'd booked and paid for the weekend. Especially since he'd travelled all the way here. We had the room available, and it is just one guy. I don't mind looking after him."

Joanne didn't look too happy about this turn of events, but she sighed and shrugged, resigned to the fact there was nothing she could do.

"It's fine, Dominic. You did the right thing. I would be furious if I'd shown up at a bed-and-breakfast I'd booked and paid for in good faith, only to be turned away because the owners were having a party. You're right, it is only one guest, but I was hoping we'd be able to have a relaxed weekend without any work."

"Actually," Dominic said. "I did tell him what was going on and he said he wasn't expecting anyone to be at his beck and call. He just wanted to enjoy the private beach. He seems pretty low maintenance."

"That doesn't sound too bad," Lilly said. "You have a whole compliment of staff and only one guest. It could be worse. Especially if he's being so understanding about the mix up."

"Yes, you're right. And there's certainly enough people to help him so Robert and I can enjoy our celebration. Come on, let's continue the tour, then I'll mix us a gin and tonic."

Lilly followed Joanne downstairs while Dominic continued his duties.

NATALIE SAMPSON MET them at the base of the stairs and gave Lilly her room key, saying she was looking forward to learning more about tea over the weekend. She then disappeared to help Dominic with the room preparations. Even though they weren't to be used over the weekend, as soon as the festivities were over The Palms was booked solid throughout the whole of the summer and well into the autumn, Joanne told Lilly. Preparing it all now meant everyone would be able to take some much needed time off.

Lilly and Joanne made their way to the dining room, where she met the elderly cook, Morris.

"And who is the gorgeous young lady?" he said by way of a greeting, which included quite a naughty wink.

Lilly laughed. "It's nice to meet you, Morris," she said, shaking the old man's hand.

"You too, my dear," he chuckled, as he continued to clean and polish the large oak dining table. "Joanne, have you heard from your husband about Jack? Is he coming this weekend?"

Joanne nodded. "Yes, he is coming, Morris, but I don't want you to get your hopes up too much."

"Who's Jack?" Lilly asked curiously.

"Robert's father," Joanne said. "He and Morris served together in the army." She smiled affectionately at the old cook.

"So, Jack has lost some more marbles then?"

"Morris!" Joanne exclaimed. "That's no way to talk about your old friend."

"Nonsense, Joanne. That's exactly what Jack would have said if the roles were reversed and I had Alzheimer's. You know I love that man like a brother and would do anything for him. Besides, you can't take life too seriously when you get to our age."

"You always seem to bring Jack out of his trances when you're together, Morris. I hope you manage it this weekend. I know it would make Robert happy if he could see a bit of the father he remembers shining through."

"Challenge accepted," he said before giving both women a salute, collecting his cleaning supplies, and disappearing into the kitchen.

"He seems like a fun person to have around," Lilly said. "I'm sorry to hear about Robert's father. Is it serious?"

"I'm afraid so. His moments of lucidity are very rare now. I don't think he's going to be with us for much longer," Joanne admitted. "But he did tell Robert he was looking forward to coming here this weekend, which is a lot more conversation than we usually get from him. Robert obviously caught him on a good day. Now, let's see, you haven't seen the gardens yet. You need to meet Walter. He's our gardener, handyman, and can turn his attention to most things. Which is a godsend when things break for no apparent reason. You'll like him. I think he's outside. Come on..."

Joanne took Lilly out of a side entrance which led straight to the formal flower gardens where guests had Tiffin each afternoon. It went right up to the edge of the cliff, a white picket fence being the only thing separating them from the sheer drop to the beach and sea below. In the midst of the garden were a number of tables with large umbrellas where they would be having the celebration over the course of the weekend. In one corner of the large oasis, she spied a man crouched over the dirt, putting in some colourful Azaleas.

Tiffin & Tragedy

"Oh, Walter, these are going to look stunning when they've grown a bit," Joanne said, approaching the man who, upon hearing his name, stood up to greet them.

"I think so too. I'm sorry we lost the old ones over the winter. I wasn't expecting the ground frost we got. Killed the roots off." He then noticed Lilly and offered her a warm smile. "Walter," he said, introducing himself.

"Lillian. But everyone calls me Lilly."

"One of my favourite names," he said, putting a soil laden gloved hand to his chest in dramatic fashion. "It's the gardener in me, I can't resist a girl named after a flower." He pointed to the tall slender stems with vibrant purple, orange and yellow flowers adjacent to the fence. "Those are our lilies. They've been strong this season and have lasted long past their normal blooming time. They're positively glowing this year, so you're getting a special treat."

"They are very beautiful," Lilly said. "Especially against the white of the fence."

"Joanne? Where are you?" a familiar voice called.

"Oh, brilliant. Robert and Chloe are back." Joanne said excitedly, making her way round to the front of the house. Lilly followed after complimenting Walter on his handiwork in the garden.

As she walked, Lilly pulled out her phone, intending to send a text to Stacey.

"There's no mobile service out here, I'm afraid, Lilly," Robert said when he spotted her.

Lilly put the phone back in her pocket. "It's all right, I'll send an email later."

She took in the sight of Robert as she approached. He looked like he'd lost a bit of weight and grown his hair slightly since she'd last seen him. He was a family man at heart and it was clear the intervening years had been as kind to him as they had to Joanne. They both looked as though they were thriving at The Palms.

She smiled when she saw Joanne hurry to her husband and give him a fierce hug, as though they'd been apart for days rather than a few hours.

"It's so good to see you, Lilly," Robert said, giving her a brief hug, too. "I'm really glad you were able to come this weekend." He turned towards a young lady who was just getting out of the car. "Chloe, do you remember, Lilly?"

The teenage girl's eyes widened slightly. Then she grinned. "Yes, I think so," she replied, getting pulled into a hug by her father as she walked past.

"Let me tell you, Lilly," Robert said. "I feel as though I've been living in paradise these last few years, with my two favourite girls."

"Dad..." Chloe groaned, embarrassed. But Lilly could see she was fighting back a smile.

"Seriously, I don't know what my life would be like right now if I had written to you."

Lilly beamed. "I'm sure you would have worked it out, Robert. But I'm really happy to be here to celebrate with you. This place really does look like paradise."

The four of them made their way back inside, chatting about the plans for the upcoming party.

Chapter Three

WITH THE BED-AND-BREAKFAST almost deserted, apart from staff and family members due to the party, Lilly spent her time enjoying what it had to offer. Plenty of strolls on the beach, swims in the sea, afternoon tea and board games in the evening for them all. It almost felt like old times, Lilly recalled, as during their early engagement Joanne and Robert would frequently hold small social gatherings like this.

Because of the relaxed atmosphere, Lilly felt as though she'd come to know the staff quite well, which would have been almost impossible if it had have been full of guests. Natalie Sampson was lovely, with a great personality, as well as being a very attractive woman. She kept the place clean and tidy, but was far from being a stickler. She played a few practical jokes on Chloe as the two of them seemed to be in the middle of a prank competition.

Walter, still enamoured by her name, brought her flowers. On her first morning she found he'd even taken the time to put a display of lilies on the breakfast table. He was certainly a hard worker, but very thoughtful, too. Constantly wandering the gardens in an attempt to make every flower pot, hanging basket, shrub, bush and patch of lawn perfect. He was managing it too, Lilly thought. It all looked absolutely stunning, and the fragrances were gorgeous.

Morris entertained them all with war stories during dinner. They'd obviously been told many times before, but Lilly's presence was a good excuse to repeat them. Apparently, Robert's father Jack had taken a bullet during the time they'd served together, a bullet meant for Morris thus saving his life. It was a riveting tale of bravery and survival against the odds, and Lilly was enraptured.

And Joanne's nephew Dominic, handsome and sprightly, decided to erect both a volleyball net and a boules pitch on the beach as additional entertainment for Lilly. She had the impression all the staff were as much a part of the family as the real members. They all got along well and truly enjoyed one another's company.

The day before the party, Lilly and Joanne scurried about putting up decorations and displaying the elegant and very stylish tea set Lilly had brought for them. It was being used mostly as decor, displayed on the garden table.

"Oh, Lilly, you know me so well. It's just beautiful. Thank you so much."

The design was one Lilly knew Joanne, with her love of vintage, would like. The teapot had a pale pink body with a lid, spout, and handle, all in white and decorated with vintage roses. Gold accents completed the look and Lilly had to admit, along with the coordinating tea cups, milk jug, sugar bowl and spoons with matching handles, it looked stunning as the display centrepiece.

"You really have an eye for this sort of thing, Lilly," Joanne continued. "And Walter is going to add displays of tea roses and lilies. I'll serve champagne cocktails and Pimms in the other teacups I have, and I thought Morris could do some cupcakes using the colours of your tea set. What do you think of pale pink butter-cream with a darker pink icing rose on top?"

"They sound perfect. It's going to be amazing, Joanne," Lilly said as the two of them made their way to the front of the house, where they heard the sounds of a car pulling up.

"Robert," Joanne called out. "It looks like your sister is here, with your dad."

They met the large car as it came to a stop and parked on the front drive, with Robert and Chloe joining them a moment later, just as the driver stepped out.

He was a tall, heavily built man with a sour expression and for some reason Lilly immediately felt unnerved. The deep frown lines on his forehead and the sullen set of his mouth seemed to suggest that smiling was a rarity. Robert and his family seemingly ignored the man's mood, so she suspected this was his usual countenance. They greeted him, sounding as friendly as they always did.

"Hi, John, how was the drive?" Robert asked with a smile.

John just huffed in response. Robert shook his head and moved to the passenger side, opening the car door for his sister, Sarah. Lilly smiled. She remembered meeting Sarah at the wedding five years before. Sarah yawned and thanked her brother for opening the door.

"Gosh, it's good to be home," she said. "Can you help me with dad, Robert?"

Lilly stood by, watching as John, evidently Sarah's husband, lurched up the steps to the front door of the property without offering any assistance, while Robert retrieved the wheelchair from the boot. John let the house door slam shut without so much as a glance behind him. He hadn't even bothered to introduce himself to Lilly. He'd just walked past, ignoring her.

Granddad Jack was in the back seat of the car. Robert had slid open the side door, but Jack didn't seem to have noticed the car had even come to a halt, let alone that his children, Robert and Sarah, were gently trying to manoeuvre him out and into the waiting wheelchair.

"Is there anything I can do to help?" Lilly asked Joanne softly while Chloe stood next to the car talking animatedly to her granddad. Jack, in return, gave no acknowledgment that he either understood or was aware of what was happening around him. Just a confused and vacant stare in her general direction.

Joanne shook her head. "It's better if they do it. Robert and Sarah have it down to a fine art now. He's old, Lilly, with both a body and a mind that's failing him. He's mostly confused and hardly knows if he's on this earth or Fuller's most of the time. I'm surprised he wanted to come, actually. But I'm glad he has." She lowered her voice. "Robert's mother was going to come too, but honestly, it's been very hard on her recently, both physically and emotionally. She did want to be here to help us celebrate, but Robert and Sarah decided to surprise her with a spa weekend break. It was Morris's idea, actually. It's a full-time job taking care of her husband now, so we're all pitching in to help with Jack so she can have a bit of a breather. She's had her hands full, especially lately as unfortunately he's taken a turn for the worse. I think it will be good for her to have some time for herself."

Lilly nodded. She had always thought Robert was a good and caring person, so to hear he and his sister had planned something nice for their mother didn't come as a surprise. She glanced back at the house with a slight frown, which Joanne immediately interpreted correctly.

"That's typical John for you. Don't take anything he says or does personally, he's all talk and no walk if you know what I mean, and doesn't get on with anyone, really."

"It was a long drive," Sarah said, obviously having overheard the comments about her husband and not looking pleased about them. "You know how John hates long car journeys."

"Well, we appreciate you both going to get Jack, Sarah. It was very kind of you," Joanne said, then looked down at the old man in the wheelchair. "Hello, Jack, I'm so glad you're here." She bent to give him a kiss on the cheek.

"Veronica," he replied breathlessly, using the name of Robert's first wife, Chloe's mother.

Chloe frowned. "No, Granddad, this is Joanne. Mum's not with us anymore, remember?"

"It's all right, Chloe. Let's get inside, shall we? We were about to start lunch so your timing is perfect."

THEY ALL MADE their way inside to the dining room where John was already seated and stuffing his face with some of the food Morris and Dominic were bringing out from the kitchen.

"Honestly, John," Sarah said in exasperated tones. "Couldn't you have waited just five minutes for the rest of us?"

"Oh, shut up, I'm hungry." John scowled as everyone else started to take seats. Dominic started to sit, but John waved a hand at him. "Before you sit down, get everyone a drink. You work here, remember?"

Dominic frowned, and his face reddened slightly. "Yes, okay. Sorry," he said.

By the look on Dominic's face, Lilly suspected this was John's typical behaviour and attitude.

"I'll do it, Dominic," Morris said. "You sit down with your family."

John glared at Morris. "I told Dominic to do it, Morris. He's got to learn that just because he's Joanne's family doesn't mean he's not one of our employees. He doesn't get special treatment just because he's related to Robert's wife."

Lilly had almost forgotten that Robert's sister was part owner of The Palms and by extension her husband obviously had some authority over the staff. They weren't present when she'd arrived and it had slipped her mind. From what she understood, Robert and Sarah had taken over the place from their father and their spouses had come to work alongside them.

"It's fine," Dominic said quickly, and Lilly was under the impression he wanted to avoid a confrontation with John at all costs. And glancing around the table, it was obvious no one else seemed to want to get involved either. "I'll get drinks for everyone, don't worry, Morris," Dominic finished.

The atmosphere was filled with a mild tension while the drinks order was filled, but Morris tried valiantly to diffuse the situation by chatting to Jack about their time during the Falkland's conflict. Jack managed the odd smile, but his responses were slight, apart from the odd nod of his head. According to the whispers from Joanne, who was seated next to her, this was more than they had expected. As Morris continued regaling them with humourous stories of their time together, he managed to make the old man smile, and once he laughed at an inside joke. Morris's presence seemed to bring a bit of light to Jack's eyes, as though he were snapping back into reality, if only for a brief moment.

"It's down to Jack that you came to work here. Do I have that right, Morris?" Lilly asked while the group was enjoying their lunch.

"Yes, that's right, Lilly," Morris said with a grin. "After Sarah and Robert took over, along with their partners, they were looking for a new cook. The Palms was a little understaffed at the time because Jack did most of the work himself. Jack put a good word in for me. Isn't that right, Jack?"

Jack smiled and nodded, although Lilly could see he was nodding at the sound of his name rather than any understanding of the question. He slumped back into his wheelchair and was once more lost in a world of his own.

"I was going through a bit of a bad time then," Morris continued. "I was homeless. War does bad things to a man and I couldn't settle when I got back. If it wasn't for Jack's recommendation and Robert and Sarah's kindness in offering me a chance, I don't know where I'd be right now. This place saved me. It's life changing having the right sort of people in your corner."

"Well, you are obviously good at what you do, Morris, and I can see you love working here," Lilly said.

"More than anything. And I get to see this old reprobate once in a while, too," he said, squeezing Jack's shoulder. "Didn't you mention some new medicine Jack's trying, Robert?"

John scoffed. "For all the good its doing. He's about as alert as ever. It's like talking to a wall most of the time."

"John, don't... please," Sarah muttered, looking both mortified and weary at her husband's attitude.

"I'm just telling it like it is, Sarah. Your mother is spending all that money on experimental drugs and it's obvious they aren't working. I'm not trying to upset you, but he's getting old, and it's time to face facts."

Chloe sighed loudly, staring daggers at her uncle.

"Something you want to say, Chloe?"

"No."

"No, what?"

"No, I haven't anything to say," Chloe responded defiantly, folding her arms and meeting John's steely gaze with one of her own.

John rolled his eyes. "Stop trying to be clever, Chloe. It doesn't suit you. And have a bit more respect for your elders.

Right, I'm exhausted after that drive, I'm going to crash out for a while." He stood, and throwing his napkin on his plate, left the room to an audible sigh of relief from Robert.

"I hate him!" Chloe announced to gasps from Robert and Joanne.

"Chloe!" they both exclaimed at once.

"Well, I do. I don't know why Aunt Sarah married him, he's horrible."

"That's enough, Chloe. Apologise to your Aunt," Robert said.

Sarah shook her head. "It's all right, Robert. Chloe, I married him because I love him. You'll understand when you're older. I know he's difficult sometimes, but he's had a long day and is tired. try to understand, okay?"

Chloe nodded. "Okay. And... sorry."

Sarah leaned across the table and squeezed her niece's hand.

"So, do you and John live here too, Sarah?" Lilly asked. "I know Robert, Joanne and Chloe have their own suite here."

"Yes, we have our own suite, too. John oversees the hiring and purchasing. I do most of the bookings and scheduling. And Robert and Joanne do almost everything else, if I'm honest," she laughed. "They are actually the brains behind the whole operation. I don't think John and I would have been able to make it such a success on our own."

"Speaking of bookings," Joanne said. "We currently have a guest staying. He arrived earlier. I don't suppose you accidentally took a booking, did you?"

Sarah covered her face. "Oh, no. Please tell me I didn't do that." She groaned at that thought of making such a slip up on what was supposed to be her brother- and sister-in-law's special weekend.

"Honestly, it's no problem, Sarah, I was just trying to work out how it happened."

"Yes, it might have been me," Sarah admitted. "Last week was a bit chaotic. There was more than our usual amount of enquiries for summer bookings, which is great for the business, but that one might have slipped through. I'm so sorry."

"Seriously, it's fine. One guest won't be a problem to look after. Don't worry about it."

Sarah sighed, brushing off the error with a wry smile, then turned to Dominic. "So, I hear your mum and brother are coming this weekend?"

"Yes. They'll be here tomorrow. Mum's really looking forward to seeing you."

Joanne explained to Lilly how Sarah and her other sister-in-law, Fiona, Dominic's mother, became close when Joanne's brother died. "Sarah became a real tower of strength and support for Fiona, when I was in the midst of grief myself."

Dominic nodded in agreement. "You and Robert getting together did a lot for both families, Joanne."

Lilly smiled. She was glad to realise she had had a hand in the resulting happiness of this lovely group of people.

Chapter Four

IT WAS THE morning of the anniversary celebration and Lilly was very much looking forward to it all. She had a shower and then put on shorts and a loose fitting tee shirt suitable for the heat of the day, before trotting downstairs to the dining room. She knew it would be a busy few hours to get everything ready before she could relax and enjoy herself, so she wanted to make the most of a hearty breakfast to set her up in case they needed to work through lunch.

When she arrived, there was only one other person seated and she didn't recognise him.

"Good morning," he said pleasantly, flipping casually through a newspaper while enjoying tea, freshly squeezed orange juice and a delicious-looking continental breakfast.

"Good morning," she replied, sitting down just as Dominic appeared by her side.

"Good morning, Lilly. Did you sleep well?"

"I did, Dominic, thank you. That bed is the most comfortable one I've ever slept in. And it was lovely listening to the sound of the sea gently breaking on the shore. Almost hypnotic. It certainly put me to sleep."

"It has that effect on a lot of guests. Now, what would you like for breakfast?"

Lilly glanced at what the stranger had chosen. Muesli, fresh fruit, croissants with homemade jam and creamy butter, a pot of tea and a tall glass of juice.

"I'll have what this gentleman is having, please. It looks delicious."

Dominic disappeared, and Lilly turned to the other guest. He'd put his paper down and was smiling at her.

"I don't believe we've met," Lilly said. "How do you know Robert and Joanne?"

"I don't. Not really," he said with a wry smile. "I'm the guest who booked a room during a family weekend celebration."

"Oh," Lilly said, with a laugh. "I'm sorry. I didn't mean to bother you. I assumed you were here for the party."

"It's quite all right. I'm just doing my best to stay out of everyone's way. As well as feeling very grateful I wasn't asked to leave as soon as I got here."

Lilly shook her head. "They would never have done that. It's hardly your fault, you didn't know. It was an oversight by one of the owners, I believe. You've been very understanding about the whole thing. It's very kind of you."

"It's a special weekend, and they have been very accommodating. I'm, Sam, by the way," he said, reaching across the table to shake her hand.

"Lillian, but please call me, Lilly, everyone does."

"A pleasure, Lilly. It's actually fun being here with a celebration planned. Robert was even kind enough to invite me to this evening's festivities, considering I'm not on the official guest list. I think he feels a bit awkward and doesn't know what to do with me. I've told him not to worry. I'm here to get away for a while, to enjoy the private beach and generally relax. I'm quite happy with my own company and don't require any special treatment."

"Is it the first time you've stayed here?" Lilly asked, pouring milk onto the cereal Dominic had just brought to her.

"Oh, no, not at all. As a matter of fact, I've been holidaying here since I was a boy. I've seen the place go through a number of owners over the years. I can remember coming here with my grandparents as a child and collecting shells, building sandcastles on the beach and catching minnows in the rock pools. I don't come as often as I like nowadays, but it's nice to take a trip down memory lane every now and again."

"That's a lovely story," Lilly said. "And talking of stories, I bet you could tell a few about this place, considering you've known it for so long?"

Sam grinned. "I could probably tell you more than you'd care to know." He ate the last bite of his croissant, dabbed his mouth with the napkin, then rose. "But, perhaps another time. I'm going to enjoy the beach this morning while I have it to myself. Enjoy your stay, Miss Tweed. And be careful if you explore the place on your own. It has many little secrets. We wouldn't want you to get lost now, would we?"

And with that friendly, but strangely ominous parting shot, Sam left the room. Lilly stared after him as a thought struck her. She hadn't told Sam her last name was Tweed.

WHEN DOMINIC BROUGHT the rest of her breakfast, Lilly asked him what he could tell her about Sam?

He shrugged, laying assorted dishes in front of her. "Not much really. He's a regular customer. Comes a couple of times a year in the summer and once in the winter, too. Although I think it's been a little while since his last stay. I know he's mentioned knowing the owners before Robert's dad bought it, which was years ago."

"I see. He's a bit, I don't know, odd."

"A little, maybe, but he's harmless," Dominic assured her. "I think he likes being in the know about the building and its history. He's really sentimental about the place. He knows a lot more about it than Robert or Sarah."

"Dominic." A woman's voice said from the door.

Lilly turned in her seat to see a slim woman enter, wearing crop jeans and a blue and white striped tee shirt. Navy deck shoes and sunglasses nestled in a riot of short dark curls completed the look. She looked extremely weary from travelling. Right behind her was a young man who, apart from a few minor facial features, looked exactly like Dominic. It was such a startling similarity Lilly paused for a moment, doing a double take. She vaguely recognised the woman from the wedding, but not the young man with her, although it was obvious who they both were.

"Mum, you made it," Dominic said, giving her a hug. "Have you both eaten? I can ask Morris to get you breakfast."

"Sounds great," Dominic's brother said. "You know what I like."

"The usual, mum?"

"Please, dear. Can you join us?" she asked, then in an added whisper, "John's not around, is he?" which seemed to suggest to Lilly she knew about the man's difficult disposition. Especially when it came to staff taking time off. Even when it was supposed to be a friends' and family weekend.

"Forget him, mum. I don't think Robert would mind, considering our only guest has just finished," he replied, clearing Sam's breakfast things away and returning to the kitchen.

The woman and her son sat at the table and she turned to Lilly. "I don't believe we've met?"

"Lilly Tweed. You must be Fiona, Joanne's sister-in-law?"

"Yes, that's right," Fiona said. "And you must be the agony aunt who brought our two love birds together?"

"Yes, that's me."

"You've obviously met Dominic. This is my other son, Edward."

"It's nice to meet you. I hope you don't mind but I have to ask, are you and Dominic twins?"

"Irish twins," Edward said. "I'm the eldest by ten months."

"Wow, you must be superwoman," Lilly said to Fiona.

Fiona laughed. "I can tell I'm going to like you, Lilly," she said.

Dominic arrived back a few minutes later with breakfast for himself and his family. He sat across from his brother and smiled. "Good to see you, Ed."

"You too, little brother. You'd better be careful John doesn't see you sitting with us when you should be working."

"John can go to..."

"Dominic! John is as much your boss as your Aunt Joanne."

"Am I right in thinking it was Jack who first bought The Palms?" Lilly said.

"That's right," Fiona said. "He bought it shortly after he left the army. Fixed it up and was running it almost single handedly for a while, with his wife helping part time. Unfortunately, he didn't have it for long. He damaged his back falling off a ladder while working in the grounds, and he hit his head on a rock as he landed from what I understand. He wasn't able to keep up with it after that. Robert, Sarah, and John took over and hired Walter to help. He's been working here ever since Jack had his accident."

"It must have been quite a while ago?" Lilly said.

"About ten years now. Robert and Sarah have worked wonders here. I've seen pictures of what it looked like before and you'd hardly recognise the place. Then five years ago Robert married Joanne and with her background in marketing and her eye for interior decorating she really helped it grow. Needing additional staff as it became more and more popular, my boys came to work here."

"So, you used to work here too, Edward?" Lilly asked, to bring him into the conversation. She already knew he had from Dominic.

Edward huffed. "Yeah. I was fired."

Fiona squeezed his arm. "Let's not rake over old coals, Edward. It's done. How about we forget about it?"

"So, I understand you and Joanne are sisters-in-law?" Lilly said, trying to get the family relationships straight in her mind.

"Yes, Joanne's brother is my late husband."

Lilly nodded. "I'm sorry for your loss."

"It was a few years ago. Cancer. It was a really hard time for me and the boys. But I think we're finally beginning to bounce back a bit."

The clicking of the silverware on plates was the only sound from the brothers as they ate, each with their own thoughts at the mention of the father they'd lost.

"I understand you and Sarah are good friends?"

Fiona smiled. "The best. I got to know her when the boys started working here, but she was an absolute godsend and a tower of strength when my husband was sick. I don't know how I would have managed without her."

"I'm glad you had someone to turn to," Lilly said, buttering her last croissant.

"You know, I really should thank you for helping Robert and Joanne find each other. I would never have met Robert and his sister otherwise. And I've become such good friends with Sarah over the years. Your advice not only resulted in a perfect match, but an important friendship as well. Plus Edward and Dominic have become close to Robert, and I know Dominic adores working here. So, thank you, Lilly."

"My pleasure. It's a shame I'm just now playing catch-up with them both. I haven't seen them both since the wedding, although we've spoken on the phone and exchanged emails and cards. It really is wonderful being here and seeing them both and Chloe, and what a fantastic job they've done with this place. It's really beautiful and very sympathetically restored."

"It is. Although truthfully it's been a while since I've been here myself."

"What mum means," Edward said. "Is that she has been avoiding the place ever since John fired me."

"Oh, Edward, please can we not do this now, darling? I know you're angry and frustrated, but this weekend is supposed to be about celebrating with Joanne and Robert. It's not about you or what has gone on in the past, wrong as it may have been."

"I know, mum, I'm joking. *Mostly*," he added.

Dominic grinned and made a few sarcastic, but humourous comments about his brother not being able to keep his job, which was responded to by Edward issuing a warning that it was only a matter of time before Sarah's grouchy husband got rid of him too.

AFTER BREAKFAST, LILLY went in search of Joanne to see what else needed doing in preparation for the party. She had a small list, but it seemed for the most part Lilly's role was already completed. Joanne asked Lilly if she'd help Walter in the garden, selecting flowers for the arrangements accompanying the displays and the central table decorations, but after that small task was completed Joanne insisted she relax.

"I want you to be able to enjoy the party and your break too," Joanne said. "I know I asked you to come early to help a bit, but that was mainly so I could spend some time with you before everyone else arrived. We've got most of it done now. Why don't you have the rest of the day to yourself, explore the place?"

Lilly admitted she'd love to, but on the proviso that should there be anything else she could help with, Joanne was to promise to let her know.

She decided to take a walk through the grounds and enjoy the scenery. The Palms was situated in isolation with no near neighbours, on several acres of land stretching for a few miles from its perch on the cliff. The beach with its ocean vista was only one of many stunning scenes the Bed and Breakfast had to offer.

Further from the more orderly and structured recreation gardens there were orchards providing seasonal fruits for the kitchen, and a kitchen garden and greenhouses tucked out of the way provided vegetables and salad stuff. She loved the self sufficiency of it all. But beyond that, Lilly found herself on a wilder path leading to a large woodland area, which reminded her of home. She walked for several minutes through the dappled shade of the trees before realising if she continued, it was very likely she would get lost. There was talk of providing a woodland trail for guests at some point in the future, so Joanne had told her, and Lilly imagined it would be a success, however it would be foolhardy for her to continue today without a guide.

She turned to retrace her steps and as she was approaching a small grassy glade she spied two white-tailed deer, a mother and fawn. She hid behind a tree and quietly took several photographs on her phone. After several captivating minutes of watching them munch on the grass, a sound which Lilly didn't hear spooked them and they bounded away.

Lilly continued her journey back to the bed-and-breakfast, thrilled to have witnessed such a unique and beautiful sight. She attempted to send a picture of the deer and a quick message to Stacey, knowing she'd be interested, but frustratingly there was no mobile phone signal. She made a mental note to email her later from her room.

For the rest of the day, friends started trickling in to help Robert and Joanne celebrate their anniversary and to enjoy the beach and other amenities The Palms offered before the party began in earnest that evening.

Chapter Five

THE FORMAL GARDENS looked absolutely amazing. Joanne and Lilly had strung up paper lanterns around the picnic table umbrellas, fairy lights in among the trees, bushes and along the fence cordoning off the drop to the beach. Candles were placed on the tables in small cranberry glasses and torch effect solar lights edged the lawns and pathways. Festive fabric bunting was strung up on just about every available surface. It looked like the set of a fairytale.

Lilly had changed into a calf length dress for the evening festivities, cream cabbage roses with Myrtle and Moss green leaves on a pale tea green background, and paired it with cream sandals. The look was finished by a three strand necklace of pearls and matching ear-rings.

Joanne's sister-in-law, Fiona, had surprised the couple with a beautiful cake, a smaller replica of their wedding cake.

Lilly had set it in pride of place on the display table, which now housed numerous gifts to be opened by the couple in private. It made for a perfect addition and really brought the whole thing together.

There was a slide show Chloe had put together of her dad and step mum during their last five years together, and judging from the laughs and whispers, some of the images Robert and Joanne had never seen. It made the show more personal and enjoyable. It was very special.

As people began to move to the dance area, a large wooden floor with several posts strung with fairy lights, to take advantage of the music playing through the speaker system Walter had set up that afternoon, Lilly stood and made her way over to the cliff side.

"The weather has been perfect for their celebration so far, hasn't it?" Sam said as Lilly joined him to gaze across the expanse of water. "Though I did hear it was due to change. I'm afraid we could be in for some high winds before long."

"I think we can cope with a bit of high wind as long as it doesn't spoil their anniversary party," Lilly said. "I hope you're not feeling too out of place here, Sam."

"Not at all. I don't know the owners well enough to have merited a legitimate invitation, but I can't fault their hospitality. Free drinks, a fabulous buffet and some excellent tea. What more could a man wish for?" he said with a laugh. "Although I do think it's time I called it a night, it's getting late. I'm looking forward to a bit of quiet time in my suite. I came here to relax after all."

As Sam wished her goodnight and retired to his rooms, Lilly returned to the main party. It had been a huge success, although she noted, as Sam had predicted, the wind was beginning to pick up. Guests, realising the weather was about to turn, said their goodbyes and thanks to the happy couple and hastily began to depart.

As they waved to the last of them, the wind increased substantially and the rain started. Not a soft trickle, but a huge sudden downpour that took everyone by surprise and drenched them through within seconds. It was all hands on deck as they rushed around, trying to salvage the equipment, food, crockery and gifts before it was ruined.

Chloe rushed to bring in the apparatus from the slide show while others snagged decorations. Walter and Morris made light work of taking down the sound equipment and getting it safely into storage in the barn.

A tablecloth escaped as Lilly was running towards the terrace, taking to the air like an out-of-control kite and heading towards the cliff. She and Sarah both darted after it, though Sarah managed to grab it first before it was lost forever.

"Close call, Sarah. You were very quick there."

"Would you believe I used to be a runner? It was a long time ago though."

Lilly could hardly hear a word she was saying due to the howling wind. "I'm getting soaked. Come on," she shouted, grabbing Sarah's wrist and trying to make herself heard.

The two of them threw the tablecloth over their heads in an attempt to shield themselves from the deluge while they sprinted back to the building. They were the last ones to come running through the door into the main living area, laughing at themselves for putting so much effort into saving a tablecloth, and assuming a sodden piece of fabric would prevent them from getting wet.

"Oh, very smart, Sarah," John said with an unpleasant scowl. "You got yourself soaked chasing after a stupid tablecloth."

Lilly immediately felt indignation at John's comment. If he was casting aspersions on Sarah, then he was inadvertently accusing her of being a fool too.

"You're just as soaked as we are," she said, a tad sarcastically. "Look at the puddle you're standing in."

John looked down and swore under his breath. "These are new shoes. Now they're ruined."

"I can't believe this storm," Sarah said. "It was supposed to be a few high winds, but nothing like this deluge."

"Those weather people never get anything right, you know that," John said, bending to remove his shoes. "They should be ashamed of themselves."

"I suppose it's just a freak storm," Lilly said, handing the cloth to Sarah to wring out ready for the laundry. It was then she noticed the bruise around her wrist. "Oh, Sarah, how did that happen? It wasn't me when I grabbed your wrist, was it? I'm so sorry."

Sarah pulled her sleeve down and shook her head. "No, don't worry, it wasn't you. I'm a bit accident prone, that's all." She laughed.

"I keep telling her to be careful, she bruises easily," John said.

Lilly frowned, noting that John was staring at her intently, as though challenging her to contradict him. Sarah, on the other hand, was busying herself with the cloth and doing everything she could to avoid meeting her gaze. It left an unsettling feeling in the pit of Lilly's stomach.

But before anything more could be said, a deafening roar of thunder followed immediately by a bolt of lightening, which seemed to light up the whole world for a second, made everyone jump in fright. Then the place was plunged into darkness as the power went out.

"Ow. Blast it," Morris said, bumping into a coffee table.

"Oh no, the power has gone off," Edward groaned.

"Well done, Ed. You have a real knack for stating the obvious. I tell you, if brains were bird droppings you'd have a clean cage."

"John, please," Sarah said.

"Everybody stay calm," Robert called out over the increasing noise of family members coming to Edward's rescue. "I'll go and have a look at the fuse box and see if I can get the lights back on."

"I'll try to get the fire going. It will give us some light as well as warmth. It's getting a bit chilly in here now." Joanne said.

Someone else volunteered to find candles and with action being taken, Lilly found herself a seat near the fireplace. A moment later Fiona took another by her side.

"JOANNE, I WAS hoping I could talk to you about Edward," Fiona said. "About the possibility of him getting his job back? I know I said I wouldn't bring it up, but things have been a bit difficult at home lately. You know how much he loved working here. And he was good at the job too. The customers all loved him."

Joanne sighed and poked at the fire. "He's having a difficult time finding a job still?"

"He doesn't want to work anywhere else he wants to be with his family and his brother. Come on, Joanne, you and I both know Edward shouldn't have been sacked in the first place. John's just being his usual obnoxious self. Throwing his weight around to make himself appear the big man."

"I can't disagree. John's getting worse, actually." Joanne said. "I'll talk to Robert about it, but John does most of the hiring and firing now, unfortunately. His isn't the final call, that's up to Robert and Sarah as the owners, but you know as well as I do Sarah always takes John's side and does what he wants, which means Robert is always outvoted. My vote of course means nothing as far as John is concerned. It helps keeps the peace for Sarah, I suppose. Leave it with me, Fiona, I'll talk to them and see what I can do. But I can't promise anything, okay?"

"Thanks, Joanne. I really appreciate you trying."

By the light of the candles and the now blazing fire, Lilly watched Fiona rejoin her sons. Her curiosity piqued.

"Do you mind me asking why Edward lost his job, Joanne? I've heard it mentioned a few times since I arrived."

"I don't know all the details myself. It was a silly mistake. Something and nothing, but John decided he had to go and with Sarah taking his side, there wasn't much we could do. John would have made all our lives very difficult if he didn't get his own way, which was bad enough, but Robert was concerned he'd take it out on Sarah. To be honest, Edward is better off out of it for the moment."

"Are you and John part owners of the business, too?"

Joanne shook her head. "No, it belongs solely to Robert and Sarah. But after Robert and I got married, it was only natural that I would start working here too. I live here, Lilly, so it's my home as well. And I love the work, I really do. John didn't want anything to do with the place until I turned up. He was happy to let Sarah and Robert do all the work and just reap the benefits. But for some reason, as soon as I arrived he decided he wanted to be a part of it. Maybe he felt intimidated, or left out. I don't know."

"I see," Lilly said. "I hope you don't mind me saying, but John isn't very friendly, is he? It's as though he doesn't particularly like anyone and actually deliberately goes out of his way to antagonise them. Not a good trait for the hospitality industry, I wouldn't have thought. If I treated my customers like that, I'd lose my business pretty quickly."

"I don't mind you saying it. We all think the same. John doesn't get along with anyone." She gestured to the back of the room where he and Natalie Samson were talking and laughing. "Though Natalie has a knack for bringing out his friendlier side, as you can see. I wish she'd share her secret, it would make life a lot easier."

"Yes," Lilly said, under her breath.

Robert returned, but with the power still off, it was obvious he hadn't managed to rectify the problem.

"I'm sorry, everyone, but it looks as though we're going to be without power for the foreseeable future. I've brought torches for us all. Dominic, could you go and check in with our guest upstairs? Let Sam know we'll keep him informed, but at the moment all we can offer is company and warm fire. Take him a torch. We don't know why the power is out at the moment."

"Obviously the storm caused it, genius," John said, with a sly grin at Natalie, who grinned back as though he'd said something clever. He forced Dominic to edge past him on his way to see to Sam.

"I know that, John," Robert replied with a patience Lilly couldn't help but admire. "I just don't know what we can do about it at the moment."

"I was hoping we could play some games tonight," Joanne said.

"We still can," Chloe said. "It'll be fun in the dark with just candles and torches."

"That is not my idea of fun. I'm going to bed. Sarah, are you coming with me or are you going to sit in those soaking wet clothes and catch your death?" Lilly noticed his tone suggested it was a rhetorical question.

Sarah looked as though she wanted to stay, but reluctantly followed her husband upstairs. Other staff followed until it was just Lilly, the family and Morris left. Dominic returned shortly after, and a game of Jenga was set up at a small table beside the fire. Halfway through the game, Sam appeared.

"I'm sorry about your weekend, Sam," Robert said. "What with us booking the place for a family party and now this power cut it can't be what you hoped for."

"You can't blame yourself for the power, Robert. It's the storm. But it was getting a bit chilly, so I came to avail myself of the fire."

"Of course, help yourself. And if you want to join in the games, you're very welcome. It's almost time to get out the poker chips," Joanne said.

"Jenga!" Dominic cried as the wooden tower came crashing down, nearly knocking over a candle in the process. Edward managed to grab it just in time.

"Probably not the best game to play with candles everywhere," Sam said with a grin.

Lilly laughed. "Yes, I think it's time we moved onto cards before we burn the place down."

Robert nodded. "I agree. Joanne, could you get the cards? I think a game of blackjack is called for."

"Absolutely. Now that's what I call a proper game."

THE LATE NIGHT card games were well under way, with Lilly surprising herself by winning and amassing quite a few matchsticks and poker chips, when John came staggering back downstairs. He'd been woken by a massive crash outside. A tree had fallen as the storm picked up pace.

"There's going to be a mess for you to clear up tomorrow, Robert. I can't believe Sarah's sleeping through this racket. That tree falling nearly gave me a blasted heart attack."

"You like playing cards, John?" Lilly asked, trying to be friendly.

"Only if those poker chips are actually worth something. I play for cash."

"You know we don't play for real money, John. It's just for fun. Gambling can lead to addiction and ruin," Robert said from his seat at the card table with a quick glance at Chloe.

John had sat down on a nearby settee and now rolled his eyes. Leaning over, he tapped Jack on his arm to get the old man's attention. "What about you, Jack? I bet you had some good card games going in your army days, eh? How is it you sired such a goody two shoes son, that's what I want to know? He won't even throw a little cash on the table to play cards with his brother-in-law."

Jack glanced in John's direction and managed a half smile. John wasn't satisfied with his response, even though it was more than Jack had managed for the last few hours, Lilly thought, watching the exchange. John gave a snort. "Thanks for the support, you're a great conversationalist, you know that, Jack?"

"Don't start," Morris warned, glaring at John.

John stared him down. "Why don't you go and make us all something to eat, Morris? We've still got gas so you could do some soup. The temperature's dropped with this storm and I'm hungry."

Morris snorted and continued looking at his card hand.

"I'm not joking, Morris," John continued, with a steel edge to his voice. "You're the hired help, remember, and I'm the boss. Go and make the soup. I'll not tell you again."

Morris flushed. With anger or embarrassment Lilly couldn't tell, but he laid down his cards and headed toward the kitchen in silence. She avoided looking at John because she knew he would see the disgust in her eyes. She didn't know him, yet he'd been rude and vile to just about everyone so far. She couldn't imagine guests returning if this was the way they were treated, but she supposed he was fine with people who paid, he just reserved the vitriol for those who couldn't answer back. He was nothing more than a bully.

"Perhaps you should calm down a bit, John," Walter said, seated to Lilly's left and with a scowl she was sure matched her own.

"You too, Walter?" John snapped. "Robert, Joanne, this is what you get when you treat the help as your friends. They aren't, they are employees. This is how we get taken advantage of."

"Stop calling them 'the help' would you?" Robert snapped. "We're not living in a Victorian novel. You've got a bad attitude, John, and are spoiling the end of what has been a great day. Perhaps you'd better go upstairs. Or better still, go and help Morris in the kitchen. If you really want something to eat after the huge buffet we've just served and during a power cut, then the least you can do is hold a torch for the man." And with that, Robert picked up a torch and tossed it in John's direction.

John caught it and smirked. "What a good idea, Robert," he said, before storming away to the kitchen.

Lilly exhaled. "Blimey," she said with feeling.

"I'm sorry you've had to see John at his worst this weekend, Lilly. He wasn't happy Joanne and I planned our anniversary celebration here and lost money from paying guests. He felt we should have made plans to do it elsewhere. Though he's obviously not bright enough to realise the place would still have had to close because there'd be no one here to run it."

"I'm still here," Sam said, laughing.

"Apologies to you too, Sam. I'm more than happy to give you a full refund."

"This probably isn't what you expected from your relaxing weekend away," Joanne said.

Sam waved off the apologies. "It's all right. I've had a wonderful weekend and there's no need to refund me. It's been nice getting to know you both better for one thing. And it's your business, there's nothing wrong with using it for a family weekend. Well, I'm going to call it a night, again. I'm sure whatever Morris is cooking is delicious, but I'm exhausted."

"If you need anything, let me know," Dominic said.

"I will. Thank you. Good night, everyone."

Just as a new game of cards was starting, there came a series of almighty crashes from the kitchen.

Robert sighed and put his head in his hands. "Oh, for Pete's sake, what now?"

MORRIS CAME STORMING out of the kitchen, followed by a furious-looking John.

"Sod you, old man," John yelled, and Lilly could see he was drenched in a wet red substance. For a moment she panicked, thinking it was blood, but as he drew closer, she realised it was tomato soup.

"No, sod you, John. I've had enough. I'm leaving," Morris yelled back. "I'm going home."

"Morris!" Robert exclaimed, jumping up. "What happened?"

"Your brother-in-law is the nastiest piece of work I've ever met. You mark my words, Robert, he's going to run this place into the ground if you're not careful. And I refuse to sit here and listen to him bad mouth your father anymore. He served this country and very nearly lost his life in the process. He deserves respect. John treats him like rubbish and I'm surprised no one's bashed his nose in before now considering the vile things that come out of his mouth."

"What did John say, Morris?" Joanne said, laying a soothing hand on his arm while Morris searched in his pocket for his car keys.

"He called your dad a stupid vegetable," Morris angrily told Robert. "One of these days you're going to man up, Robert, and give the foul-mouthed pig what's coming to him. And I hope I'm here to see it."

"Morris, you can't leave. Can't you hear how bad the storm is?"

"Let him go. He just poured a pan of soup over my head, that's assault," John snapped. "We ought to sack him."

"No." Joanne shouted, turning on John. "Go and clean yourself up and go to bed, John. No one wants your nasty attitude anymore. We are not sacking Morris, and what's more I think my nephew deserves a second chance here too. You should never have sacked him in the first place. You had no good reason."

"You're out of your tiny mind. Listen, I've been part of this family a lot longer than you have, missy, and I've been through the ringer with the lot of them. You don't get to take on your family members just because you feel like it."

"Get lost, John," Joanne retorted. "Morris, Dominic and Edward all do a lot more work around here than you do."

"Joanne, calm down," Robert pleaded.

"See, that's what I mean, Robert," Morris said. "You let your brother-in-law walk all over you when you should get rid of him. He's a bad apple and one day someone will have the guts to get rid of him. I'm leaving."

"Good riddance!" John shouted.

"For heaven's sake, go upstairs and get cleaned up, John, you've done enough damage for this evening," Joanne said.

John huffed and threw up his hands. "I don't want to sit down here with you lot, anyway. Natalie, get me some towels and bring them up to room four. I don't want to wake Sarah getting cleaned up."

Natalie nodded and dashed off to do as she was ordered as John took the stairs two at a time, leaving drips of red soup on the carpet.

"Morris, please don't leave," Fiona begged, worried. "There is a violent storm raging outside. It's dangerous and the roads could be flooded. Not to mention you could be hit by a falling tree. John's not worth risking your life for. Stay here safely tonight and if you still want to leave in the morning, no one will stop you."

"Mum's right, Morris," Edward said, coming to stand by the older man. "It's really bad out there. John's gone now. Why not have a drink and play another hand with us?"

"No, I'm sorry, but that was the final straw. I refuse to stay a minute longer under the same roof as that man. I'll take my chances. I'm leaving," Morris declared, at last having found his keys. He stormed out, slamming the door in his wake.

Lilly looked out of the window, just barely able to see, as Morris's green car disappeared down the drive. She hoped he would be all right.

Chapter Six

THE FIGHT BETWEEN John and Morris and the older man's sudden departure had left an uncomfortable tension in the air, not to mention grave concern for Morris's safety. The festivities were well and truly over. After listening to several apologies from both Robert and Joanne, Lilly assured them she was fine and not to blame themselves, before retiring. The party broke up and everyone else decided to go to bed, too. Frankly, she was relieved to be alone in her room.

She felt as though she'd only been asleep for a few minutes when she was awakened by shouting. As she came out of her sleep induced haze, the shouting grew louder, accompanied by banging, and she wondered what on earth was happening. She hurriedly got out of bed, flung open the door and ran down the hall, where she found Sarah pounding on a door.

Lilly wasn't the only one who'd been awakened by the racket Sarah was making. Robert, Joanne, Chloe, Walter, Fiona, Dominic and Edward were all standing in the hallway with torches, trying in vain to calm her down.

"What's going on?" Lilly asked Chloe

"Aunt Sarah thinks John is in there with Natalie," the girl whispered.

"Really? Oh, dear…"

"Sarah, for crying out loud, please stop, you're going to wake dad up," Robert pleaded. "Not to mention our only paying guest."

"My husband is in there with our housekeeper, Robert! What do you expect me to do?" Sarah yelled. "This does it, John. I swear, you had better open this door, this minute." She shouted, pounding on the door even harder. "I knew you were having an affair. I just knew it! Natalie Sampson, when I get my hands on you I'm going to ring your cheating neck. Do you hear me? Open this door, you cowards."

"Sarah?" a voice said from the end of the hall.

Lilly turned and saw Natalie Sampson in her nightgown, walking towards them with a torch of her own. She looked as though she'd just woken up.

"What's going on?" she asked, stifling a yawn.

Sarah's face turned scarlet, and Lilly heard Joanne mutter, "Oh, Sarah," under her breath.

"Wait a minute," Natalie said, as the words Sarah had been shouting suddenly registered. "You thought I was in there? With your husband? I dropped off the towels hours ago, Sarah."

Sarah shook her head. "I... I thought you were. If you're not in there, why won't John answer me?"

"You thought I was having an affair with your husband? How dare you? How could you think such a thing?"

"I'm sorry," Sarah said tearfully. "Why won't he answer? I know he's in there." She resumed the banging on the door, shouting for John.

Lilly glanced at the number four artfully painted on the door, recalling John had gone in there to clean up after Morris had thrown soup at him. Had he not returned to his wife all night?

"Do you think something has happened?" Lilly whispered to Joanne and Robert.

"I don't know," Robert said. "Let me get the master key from reception and we'll find out."

He was gone less than a minute. He unlocked the door, only to find the security chain was in place.

"John, let us in," he shouted. When there was no reply, he rammed the door hard with his shoulder, breaking the chain and they all plunged inside.

John was laid out on the bed, multiple stab wounds apparent in his chest, blood seeping through his pajamas and onto the sheets below. Sarah screamed, her legs giving way as Dominic and Edward grabbed her and gently lowered her to the ground. Natalie shrieked and ran out of the room, collapsing in the hallway, back against the wall, in complete shock.

"John!" Robert cried out, dashing to the bed and pointlessly checking for vital signs. "He's... he's dead," he gasped, sharply pulling his hand away and turning in wide eyed shock to the others. "Dear god, what happened?"

"Looks as though someone has killed him," a voice said from the doorway, startling everyone.

Sam's eyes slowly took in the room as he observed the scene. Walking to the figure on the bed, he frowned. "Very recently too, by the looks of it."

"I'm going to call the police," Chloe said.

Sarah was sobbing. "I don't understand... what happened?"

Sam was now carefully walking around the room. Lilly watched as he tried the window. It didn't budge.

"The door was locked?" he asked the room at large. It was Fiona, from her place crouched by Sarah's side, who answered.

"Yes. Robert went for the master key then had to break it down when he discovered the security chain was in place."

Walter was pacing by the doorway. "Who would stab John?" he asked.

Sam shook his head. "I have a better question for you, Walter. How did someone manage to murder a man in a room that was locked from the inside?"

***

CHLOE CAME DASHING back into the room just as Sam's revelation hit home. Because the room wasn't in use for guests, the window had been locked and the key put safely in reception. The door had been locked from the inside. The key, Lilly saw, was sitting on the dresser to the left. The security chain had been put in place, presumably by John, in an attempt to keep everyone out. There was obviously no plausible way this could have been suicide, and considering the chaos the sheets were in, it appeared as though he'd been thrashing about in an attempt to defend himself from his attacker.

John had been murdered and the perpetrator had somehow then left a locked room. Lilly shook her head. It was utterly impossible.

Robert pulled the sheet over his brother-in-law as Chloe entered the room, not wanting her to be exposed to the gruesome scene any further.

"Dad, the landline is dead. I couldn't call the police," she said anxiously. "And there's no mobile signal or internet."

"All right, Chloe, thank you for trying," Robert said, glancing outside the window. "The storm is letting up a bit. If the phone lines are down one of us needs to get to town and bring the police back urgently."

"I'll go, Robert," Walter said immediately. "My jeep is much better in this weather than any of your smaller cars. It's likely the roads will be either washed out or slick with mud and the jeep will handle those better."

Robert nodded and clasped the man's shoulder. "Thank you, Walter. Come on, everyone, there's nothing more we can do here. We need to keep everything as it is for the police."

It was a stunned and very subdued crowd of people that made their way downstairs. Lilly was in disbelief that she had once again become embroiled in a murder investigation, and mentally made a note to arrange an appointment with Dr Jorgenson when she returned to Plumpton Mallet.

"Does anyone know what time it is?" she asked as they reached the lounge.

"About half-past three," Walter said, shrugging on his coat. "Wish me luck. It's still pretty bad out there."

"Please, be careful, Walter," Joanne said. "Don't take any risks and if you don't think you can make it turn round and come straight back."

"I promise, Joanne," he said. And taking a deep breath ventured out into the raging storm.

Lilly shuddered, imagining a roaring, violent sea churning below the cliff. One wrong turn or a loss of control on a slick road with practically no visibility, and Walter and his vehicle could easily go tumbling down into the water. It was dangerous outside, and she wondered if Walter's attempt to get to the police was foolhardy. Then she remembered the danger inside. She had to concentrate on what was happening here and hope Walter's driving experience, knowledge of the area and steadfastness would see him through.

"This is a nightmare," Sarah said, collapsing on the sofa. "I just can't believe it." She covered her face with her hands and shook her head, sobbing and trying to make sense of what had happened.

"Natalie, perhaps you'd be good enough to make us all some tea?" Sam said. "Hot and sweet for Sarah to help calm her nerves?"

For a second Natalie looked at him blankly. "There's no power?"

"A pan of water on the gas hob will work," he replied gently.

"Yes... yes, of course," she stammered. "I could do with one too. I can't stop shaking."

"Use the mint tea I brought with me, Natalie. It soothes the nerves."

"Could you help me, Lilly?"

"Of course."

The kitchen was a mess when they entered. After the altercation they'd witnessed between Morris and John, no one had remembered the soup and the hob and floor were drenched with the congealing mess.

Lilly started to clean it up while Natalie found a tray for the teapot and cups.

"Do you have any honey, Natalie? It's better than sugar."

"Yes, I'm sure we do. In the pantry. I'll go and look."

By the time Natalie came back with a jar of honey, which she put on the tray along with a spoon, Lilly had cleared up the mess and had put a pan of water on to boil.

"Are you all right, Natalie?"

"I'm not sure. I think so. Just... it's such a shock. I went from being accused of having an affair with a man, only to find him moments later murdered and covered in blood. It's a lot to take in. I'm not sure it has yet, it's unbelievable. Who would do such a thing?"

"You're doing well, Natalie. Take some deep breaths, it will help. If you don't mind me saying so, you seemed quite close to John."

Natalie wiped away a tear as she spooned mint leaves into the pot.

"If I'm honest, Sarah's accusation isn't completely without merit. John and I had become quite close recently, but not in the way Sarah suggested. Their marriage has been quite rocky, especially lately, and I think she was becoming paranoid. He wasn't the kindest of men, particularly to her, and I think her seeing him treat another woman respectfully and kindly wasn't easy. I should have kept my distance."

"I could tell their relationship had its difficulties," Lilly said, lifting the pan of boiling water and pouring it into the teapot.

With the kitchen clean and the tea made, the two women made their way back to the lounge and began to dispense the tea. Jack had now joined them. Robert had apparently heard his father stirring, having been awakened by the commotion, and had fetched him down to join the others. Lilly handed Jack his tea with a smile.

"Thank you, Daisy," he said politely.

"Close. It's Lilly," she said with a warm smile.

"Don't tease. I know you're my Daisy," Jack replied with a wag of his finger and a dazed look.

"Who is Daisy?" Lilly asked Robert quietly as she handed him a cup.

"An old girlfriend. Sorry about that, Lilly, he gets mixed up a lot nowadays."

"It's fine, Robert. I understand."

"Where's Morris?" Jack asked suddenly.

"He left last night, dad. You were here, remember?"

Jack looked momentarily confused. Then the frown turned to a vacant smile as he sipped his tea. All thoughts of Morris forgotten.

Sarah thanked Natalie and Lilly for the tea and sipped the drink slowly.

"Try to drink it all, Sarah," Fiona said.

"What the heck happened?" Robert asked, pacing back and forth. "And how? Like Sam said, the room was locked from the inside. How did someone get in there, stab John to death, then get out of the room?"

"Robert," said Joanne. "You're upsetting your sister."

"I'm all right, Joanne. It's just... well, I can't take it in, it seems unreal. Natalie, I am so sorry. I was out of line. I shouldn't have spoken to you the way I did. I wasn't thinking straight."

"There's no need to apologise, Sarah," Natalie said. "You were distraught. I honestly don't know what happened. I saw him a few hours before when I took him the towels. He seemed fine then. But what happened after that I just don't know."

They all sat quietly in the lounge sipping tea, each with their own thoughts. Trying to work out what happened and who was responsible. After about half an hour, the door opened and Walter walked in.

"It's bad news. I couldn't get to town. There are trees down all over the place and several have blocked the road. We're stuck here, I'm afraid."

"YOU'RE KIDDING ME," Robert groaned, returning to his seat next to Joanne. "How bad is it, Walter?"

"As bad as it can be. I tried going around but got the jeep stuck in the mud. It took me twenty minutes to get it out again, and I was lucky. The other side is a sheer drop off the cliff, as you know. We won't be able to clear the trees until the storm dies down. It's just too dangerous."

"Thanks for trying, Walter," Robert said. "I'm glad you got back safely. That's the main thing."

"So," Chloe said from her position next to her father. "Let me get this straight. We've got a body upstairs, murdered in a room locked from the inside, no mobile phone service, the landline is down, the police can't get here and we're trapped. Trapped with someone who killed John. Have I got all that right?"

Lilly immediately noticed a change in the atmosphere as the tension began to build. There was silence as everyone glanced suspiciously at each other, attempting to read reactions to Chloe's succinct summary of their predicament. It was true, they were trapped with a killer among them. And a clever one at that. Lilly was still getting over the shock of seeing John's dead body and she didn't even know him. She could only imagine what everyone else was thinking.

Suddenly a comment was made. Lilly didn't even know who had said it, but that was the fuse that lit the room on fire. Soon everyone was shouting accusations at one another, long held grudges, for every perceived slight, innocent or not, were dredged up and aired. Even Lilly was accused. She realised she needed to try to solve this mystery quickly before everything got out of hand and the damage to this family ended up being beyond repair. Looking at them all, she could hardly believe this was the same fun-loving group of people from the day before.

"But, Sarah," Natalie was protesting, "I already told you I didn't hurt him. How can accuse me again?"

"Well, you heard Walter, we are trapped here with a killer. It could be any one of us, including you," Sarah said, looking at Joanne for help. But Lilly could see she'd get no help there. Joanne was distraught herself, looking at her family with tears in her eyes and shock on her face.

Lilly walked over, and taking Natalie by the arm, gently guided her away from Sarah. There was a possibility this could get physical, and that was the last thing Lilly wanted to happen.

"And you," Sarah suddenly said to Lilly. "You had no right to speak to John the way you did tonight. You didn't know him. He was a wonderful husband. In fact, none of you really knew him. All of you are suspects as far as I'm concerned."

Lilly took a deep breath and held her tongue. Sarah had been through a lot this evening and it was natural she should lash out. It was also natural that at the moment she should only remember the good times rather than the violence and the abuse. She was in denial. Lilly moved to the outer edges of the family group. The better to observe. Straight heads prevailed in situations like this and she knew she must remain calm. Dominic and his brother looked to be arguing. She wondered what it was about, but going over to find out meant walking past Sarah, who was just getting into her stride.

Lilly remained in the shadows, pondering what to do as she watched another argument break out between them all.

Chapter Seven

AS LILLY WATCHED Sarah stretch to put her tea on the table, her sleeve moved and once again revealed the bruise she had noticed earlier. She realised now, due to the colouration, it was at least a few days old and she was almost certain it had been John who had been the cause. Could Sarah have been the one to kill her husband having had enough of the abuse? If that was the case, then she was doing an excellent job of acting as the bereaved wife. And how did she get out of the room?

Dominic and Edward had stopped arguing and were looking miserably at the others. Robert and Walter were discussing a plan to remove the obstructions in the road, allowing them to get to the police. And Fiona and Joanne were now trying to comfort Sarah, who was sobbing. She looked worn out and beaten down, the reality of John's death having just hit home. Pain and guilt were the next stages of grief. Natalie was standing to one side, alone and upset.

But there was one person missing.

In her peripheral vision, she saw movement and turned to find Chloe sneaking upstairs. Quietly, Lilly followed. Chloe was undoubtedly mature for her age, but she was only sixteen and still impressionable. The last place she should be was in the room with the body.

Lilly got to the top of the stairs just in time to see Chloe sneak into room four. She hurried down the hallway and stepped over the threshold.

"Chloe!" she hissed, causing the girl to jump. A guilty look on her face.

"Oh, hi."

"What are you doing in this room? Your father would be furious if he knew you'd sneaked in here. What do you think you're playing at?"

"I know, but please, Lilly, just let me explain."

Lilly looked at her for a moment, then gave a small nod. "Go on."

"Well, I thought I might be able to find something that could tell us who stabbed John. I mean, no one even looked round the room, did they? Everyone was just shocked and crying and stuff. Then we all left. I thought it would be a good idea to see if I could find some clues."

"Chloe, this isn't a game."

"I know it's not," she said, glancing quickly at the bed. "But you have experience and I know you can't be the murderer because you didn't even know him. I've read about the last two murders you solved. They were in the Plumpton

Mallet Gazette. What you did was amazing. Don't you want to try to solve this too? It could be ages until the police can get here. I could be your Watson!" she finished, eyes shining with the expectation.

"I'm not Sherlock Holmes, for goodness' sake. I'm a former agony aunt who now owns a tea shop. The cases you're talking about were mainly dumb luck, and I nearly got myself in dreadful trouble, as well as injured. I'm not a detective, Chloe, this is serious and we really need to leave it to the professionals."

Lilly was trying to work out how to get Chloe out of the room. If Robert happened to come upstairs and see them in the room together, he would be furious. And who would get the brunt of the blame? The impressionable teenager or the middle-aged adult who should know better?

"I know it's serious, that's why I came up here. No one else is doing anything except arguing and blaming each other. It's a complete nightmare downstairs. This is a total mystery, Lilly. A murderer gets away with killing someone inside a locked room and then vanishes. Please, can't we just have a quick look round and see if we can find something that would help? I've already seen the body, so it's not like you're shielding me from anything. And dad has already covered him up. Please, the quicker you help me, the quicker we can leave."

"Oh, for heavens' sake," Lilly muttered, both annoyed and reluctantly admiring the emotional blackmail. "Five minutes and no more. And if someone comes we leave and quickly. Deal?"

"Deal," Chloe said with a serious nod.

Lilly sighed. She didn't know if she wanted them to find a significant clue or not. But Chloe was right, they needed to do something. The family was tearing strips off one another downstairs.

THEY SET TO with earnest and started searching the room for anything, no matter how small, that might help them work out who the perpetrator was. Lilly didn't want Chloe anywhere near the body, so suggested she started by searching the dresser. With no guests in residence, there wasn't much in it, but Lilly was impressed by Chloe's methodical and diligent approach. She removed all the drawers, checking through the meagre contents, upended them to see if anything was stuck to the base, and looked inside the empty carcass in case something had fallen inside. There was nothing. She then moved to the wardrobe and searched it just as assiduously, but once more came up empty-handed.

Lilly searched the bedside tables and a built-in bookcase, but she too came away with nothing to show for her efforts.

"So, how did you solve your other two cases?" Chloe asked.

"They weren't my cases, but the first, like I said, was more luck than anything. I just had a feeling it wasn't the suicide the police thought it was. The second one, with some considerable help I might add, I managed to work out what the murder weapon was, which led me in the right direction."

"So we need to find the murder weapon, don't we? That would be a good start. Do you think the killer left it behind?"

"I really don't know, Chloe. It seems unlikely to me, but I suppose it would depend on how much of rush they were in and how careless. Especially if they were disturbed."

Before Lilly could stop her, Chloe rushed for the bed. She could almost hear Robert blaming her for Chloe's subsequent nightmares, but she was already too late. The girl was on her hands and knees, searching underneath.

"Wow! Look, I found something."

As it turned out, the murder weapon had indeed been left behind, thrown or kicked under the bed.

"Don't touch it, Chloe! There will be fingerprints on it. Let me find something you can use."

Lilly dashed into the bathroom and tore off a length of toilet paper, which she handed to Chloe.

"Here, use this and very carefully."

Chloe did as instructed and pushed the weapon into the open by the top edge of the pommel. Lilly could see it was a dagger of some sort, still bloodied from recent use. At the top of the blade, just below the quillon, was an engraved royal emblem; crossed swords, a crown, and a lion displayed prominently.

"An army knife?" Chloe breathed in awe.

Lilly had to agree. It was definitely military and most likely army.

"Chloe, did your granddad have this or any other army knives displayed around The Palms where someone could have just helped themselves?"

Lilly picked the knife up by the cross-guard using the paper and carefully laid it on the bedside table.

Chloe stepped closer and shook her head. "Not that I know of. I've never seen one before. But granddad wasn't the only one in the army, was he? Maybe Morris had one?"

"Morris said he was going home last night," Lilly said. "I thought all the staff lived in?"

"They do. Morris does as well most of the time, but he also has his own place in town. I think he meant he was going there." Chloe turned toward the bed and suddenly let out a gasp.

"What is it?"

Chloe reached toward the bed, and very carefully lifting up the pillow, gingerly extracting a pair of women's briefs; bright pink with black polka dots. She dropped them on the floor and looked at Lilly, aghast. "Aunt Sarah was right. He was having an affair."

While Chloe went to the bathroom to wash her hands, Lilly used her phone to take pictures of the evidence they had found so far. Thinking about the knife made Lilly sad. Morris seemed like such a nice man, very good to Jack and a hardworking and loyal member of staff. But it was John that had made Morris furious enough to leave. Had he been so angry he'd come back and killed him? She hoped not, but if there was anything her recent experiences had taught her, it was to keep an open mind.

She went to see how Chloe was doing.

"You okay, Watson?" she asked, eliciting a small smile. The girls shrugged. "Yeah, I'm fine."

"You know we can stop and leave this to police, Chloe. We've found evidence that we can pass on and let the authorities do their job."

"No, we need to keep going. We will solve it. I know we will. We have to."

"Maybe, but you need to understand you might not like what we find out. Someone in this house is responsible, Chloe. If it's not a member of staff, then it has to be a member of your family. That's going to be traumatic enough without getting involved. If we carry on and find the evidence we need, we will ultimately be responsible for unmasking a killer. The last thing I want is for you to get hurt, and I don't think you're fully prepared to deal with the fallout."

"I am, honestly. I know it's someone here, but whoever it is has to answer for what they've done, don't they? And if we can find out who it is, then maybe everyone will stop blaming each other."

The girl had a steely look in her eye, which Lilly recognised. She was not going to back down from investigating. If Lilly didn't help her, then she'd just do it on her own. The best Lilly could do was be with her and support her along the way. No matter what they found out.

"Yes, they do. All right, we'll keep going, but any time it gets too much you must tell me and we'll stop. Do you promise me?"

Chloe nodded. "I promise, Lilly."

"All right. Now, let's get out of this room and decide what to do next."

"So, we've found the murder weapon," Chloe said once they were back in the hall. "It's an army one, so either belongs to granddad or Morris. Granddad doesn't live here so I don't think it's his, and he's really ill and in a wheelchair. I also don't think he would have kept his knife here. Why would he? So I think it belongs to Morris."

"Well, Morris left last night before it happened," Lilly said. "So, who would have been able to get hold of his dagger?"

"Anyone with access to the rooms the staff live in. Which is pretty much everyone in this house."

"All right, while everyone is arguing downstairs, perhaps you and I could do a little snooping?" Lilly suggested, coming round to the idea of letting the girl help. She'd found both the murder weapon and a rather telling piece of evidence, so clearly had a keen eye as well as a determination to solve the crime. "Maybe we can see if there is anything that would indicate a quick clean up? Whoever stabbed John must have got blood on them so would have had to clean up quickly in order to get back into the hall with the rest of us. I just wish I could remember where everyone was standing, then perhaps we could work out who turned up without us noticing. But everything happened so quickly."

"Whoever it was must have killed him and got back to the hall without any blood on them or we'd have seen it. Having to do it in a rush means they could have made a mistake. There might be blood in one of the bathrooms. Come on, let's go," said Chloe.

Lilly followed Chloe to the rear of the building where the owner and employee suites were situated.

"I think we should check Natalie's room first."

"Why?" Lilly asked.

"Because it's obvious John was having an affair. It's not going to be with Joanne, so she's the only one left. But besides that, no one got along with him apart from Natalie. You must have seen the way they were with each other?"

Lilly nodded.

Reaching Natalie Sampson's room, Chloe turned the door handle but found it locked.

"We'll have to find a key," Lilly started to say before Chloe produced one from her pocket. It looked to be a master that would open all the doors in an emergency.

"Are you supposed to have that, Chloe?"

She grinned. "Nope."

Natalie's room was beautifully decorated in an ornate French style. Very feminine in blue pastel shades with cream, antique style furniture and numerous gilt-edged mirrors.

"Does it have an en-suite?" Lilly asked.

"Yes, just through there," Chloe said, pointing to a door on the left of the stunning hand decorated walnut double bed.

"I'll start there and see if there's any sign of blood. See what you can find in here."

The bathroom was relatively small, with a white suite. Lilly checked the bath, sink and shower but there were no tell tale red spots anywhere. Nothing in the waste paper bin or in the laundry basket. The cupboards above and below the sink revealed nothing more than cleaning products and cosmetics. There was no tell tale smell of bleach or other disinfectant. This was not the room where an urgent clean up had happened.

"I've found something," Chloe called out, and Lilly entered the main room to find her holding up a pink bra with black polka dots. A perfect match to the underwear they'd found under John's pillow. "It looks like Aunt Sarah was right after all."

Lilly took a photo with her phone. "So it's probable Natalie was in the room with John last night."

"Maybe they had a fight or something and she killed him?"

"But that doesn't explain how she came to have Morris's knife or how she managed to get out of a room that was locked from the inside."

"Yeah," Chloe said, frowning. "And she came up behind us in the hall, remember? If she killed John, she would have had to find a way to lock the room and get out without any of us seeing her. It's impossible. How could she have done it?"

"I think I may have the answer," a voice said from the doorway, causing Chloe and Lilly to nearly jump out of their skins. They spun round to find Sam leaning nonchalantly against the door frame.

"For crying out loud, Sam," Lilly said, breathing heavily and willing her heart to slow down.

"Sorry, I didn't mean to startle you. I've been thinking about how this could have been accomplished, and I believe I have the answer."

"You do?" Chloe said.

"Come with me," Sam said. "And be prepared for a surprise."

*L*ILLY AND CHLOE exchanged quizzical glances, but followed Sam down the hall. The opposite way to room four.

"Um, you know, John was killed in the room the other way?" Chloe said.

"Yes, I'm aware of that. But I believe Natalie exited the room from here," Sam replied, stopping in front of a large built-in bookcase.

"What?" Chloe and Lilly said together.

Sam pulled one of the lower shelves, and they all heard an audible click. The entire shelving unit then slid into the wall, leaving an opening into a tunnel. It was a door. Lilly's jaw dropped.

"A secret door!" Chloe gasped in excitement. "Oh, wow! I had no idea this was here. This place has been in my family since before I was born. How come I never knew about this?"

Sam smiled. "Like I said, this place has many secrets. I discovered it when I was a child, much younger than you Chloe. Long before your granddad bought the place." He walked inside, and Lilly and Chloe followed.

It was only a short passage and ended with another bookshelf which opened up like a regular door into room number four.

"This is amazing," Chloe said. "So this is how she did it. Natalie had some sort of argument with John. She stabbed him, but probably heard Aunt Sarah shouting and banging on the door, so slipped into this passage, cleaned up somewhere and then came walking up behind us looking like she'd just woken up."

"It's certainly a possibility," Sam said. "Although it's too early to say for sure without any proper proof."

"Well, let's go and see what she has to say about her underwear being in here, then," Chloe said, dashing back through the passage.

"Chloe, wait!" Lilly said, as she and Sam hurried after her.

The others were all still in the lounge arguing when Chloe marched up to Natalie, pointing an accusing finger.

"We know what happened. She killed John."

"Chloe," Robert admonished. "You can't just go around accusing people of murder."

Lilly bit her lip to keep from pointing out that this was exactly what he and the others had been doing for the last hour.

"There is some possible evidence," Sam said calmly. "Perhaps you could let Chloe explain?"

Robert and Joanne exchanged worried glances. Sarah got up from where she'd been sitting. "I would certainly like to hear what she has to say."

"We found your underwear under John's pillow," Chloe said. Natalie's face went white. "We know it's yours because we found the matching bra in your room."

"I knew it!" Sarah spat. "You were having an affair with my husband."

"I... we... No..." Natalie stammered as Sarah launched herself at the shaking woman and slapped her across the face. Immediately a hand shaped red welt began to bloom across Natalie's cheek.

Fiona dashed over to her friend and grabbed her arm. "Don't, Sarah. She's not worth it. And you're better than that."

Robert inserted himself between Natalie and his sister. "Calm down, Sarah. We don't know exactly what's been going on as yet."

"Natalie," Lilly said, turning to the shaken housekeeper. "Now is not the time to deny the affair. Someone killed John last night and at the moment you're the prime suspect because we know you were in the room with him."

"But I didn't kill him. Yes, we were having an affair, I'm sorry. But he was alive when I left. I promise."

"I don't believe you," Sarah yelled. "Why should I? You've been lying about the affair you could easily be lying about killing him. You're sacked. When this storm clears, I want you to pack your belongings and get out."

"Sacked?" Natalie cried and turned to Robert, expecting him to come to her defense.

"I'm sorry, Natalie, but I agree with Sarah. We can't keep you on after this. But if you are responsible, then you'll need to stay until the police can get here."

"But I didn't kill him. How could I the room was locked? And you all saw me arrive in the hall."

"That's a good point," Joanne said.

"We worked that out too," Chloe said. "There's a secret door and a passageway. You knew about it, didn't you, Natalie?"

Natalie covered her eyes and, after what seemed like an age, gave a slight nod. "But he was alive when I left. I swear."

"A secret door? Chloe, what are you talking about?" her father asked.

"Come on, I'll show you," she said, leading everyone upstairs.

Jack was left sitting in his wheelchair in front of the fire, oblivious to what was going on around him.

Once again, a flock of people descended on room four. Lilly noticed Sarah remained in the open doorway where she could still hear what was being said, but as far away as she could be from the body of her husband. Chloe showed them the bookshelf that led along a passage to the one out in the hall.

"So, I think Natalie had some sort of fight with John and stabbed him. Then left through the passage, making it appear as though she was never here," Chloe explained.

Natalie was still white and shaking but Lilly now noticed beneath the fear anger was beginning to show.

"I didn't do it. How many more times must I tell you. Yes, I slept with him, but he was alive when I left. I heard Sarah in the hall and used the passage to leave. I'm sorry I didn't mention it before, but I was terrified you'd accuse me of killing him. Just like you are now."

"I've worked here for years," Robert said. "How is it I didn't know about this passage? How did you even find it?"

"Your father showed it to me when he hired me," Natalie said. "Before his accident."

"I'm shocked at your behaviour, Natalie," Walter said.

"Oh, be quiet, Walter. I'm not the only one who knew about the passage." She turned, looking pointedly at Dominic and Edward. "I know Jack showed you two the secret doors, yet neither of you bothered to say anything when John was found. So why the silence?"

"Now wait a minute! I hope you're not trying to lay the blame for John's murder on my sons, Natalie Sampson?"

Fiona said angrily. "You're just trying to weasel your way out of this. You were sleeping with John. You were the last one to see him alive. You've got a motive. What happened? Did John try to break it off with you so you decided to kill him?"

"Let's all just take a deep breath and calm down, shall we?" Sam said in a firm tone. "I'd like to point out another piece of evidence which Chloe found. If you turn your attention to the bedside cabinet, you'll notice the murder weapon. An army dagger. Now why would Natalie have had that on her? How would she have come to be in possession of that knife? Robert, perhaps you could identify it?"

The room grew quiet as Robert made his way over to the dagger. "I remember dad having something like this when we were children. But I honestly can't say if this is his or not. I haven't seen it in years. It's definitely an army knife though. Perhaps it belongs to Morris? Sarah," he turned to his sister. "Could you have a look?"

From the doorway, Sarah shook her head. "I don't want to come in, Robert. But I wouldn't recognise it, anyway."

"Could your father identify it?" Sam asked. "As belonging to either him or Morris?"

Robert shook his head sadly. "I really don't know. The times when he is lucid are rare now. He can't walk anymore, can't dress himself. He doesn't know what's going on around him or even what day it is. He doesn't have long left, Sam. Even if we caught him on a good day and he did identify it, how would we know what he says is true? His judgment and recollections just aren't reliable. We could try I suppose, but we couldn't take what he said as fact."

Lilly had been aware of Edward's awkward shuffling since they'd entered the room. She had the feeling he was trying and failing to keep his mouth shut about something. She was proved right a moment later.

"You know, Walter knew about the passage too."

Walter glared at him, but remained silent.

"What?" Sarah said from the door. "You mean all the staff knew about this but never bothered to tell us, the owners?"

"It's always been kept as a staff secret," Walter admitted. "The Palms has been through a lot of owners over the years, as well as staff. I was told of it by Eliza, the housekeeper who retired before Natalie took over. It was her grandmother, who also worked here, I believe, who showed it to her when she was a little girl. The previous owners never knew about it either. In the olden days staff were supposed to be seen and not heard. It was a way of hiding if guests were in the hallway, or a shortcut to room four for cleaning. Many old hotels and grand houses have them."

"As I said," Sam whispered to Lilly. "There are quite a few secrets here at The Palms."

Chapter Eight

ODDLY, AS NIGHT spilled into morning and the first signs of dawn appeared outside, the tensions began to rise rather than fall. Lilly had expected everyone to begin to calm down through sheer fatigue, if nothing else, but the opposite was true. The discovery of the affair and the secret doors had added to the strain and Lilly, as an outsider looking in, could see it clearly. Unfortunately, Natalie Sampson, having now lost her job, was forced to stay as they were trapped. Trapped with a murderer and a corpse. Her presence was making the others, not least of all Sarah, irrational and resentful. It was a powder keg of emotional pressure just waiting to blow.

As the sun began to rise, a plan was worked out to attempt to clear the road in order to gain access to the town. The consensus had been that the local council were, in all likelihood, dealing with several clear ups around the area and were making the busier roads a priority. The single track up to The Palms wouldn't be high on the list, even if the authorities realised the access road was impassable. A quick check revealed the telephone lines were still down so they couldn't even call anyone to let them know.

After breakfast, leaving Chloe behind to take care of her granddad, the rest of the able-bodied adults left with various tools to help make the job easier. Armed with a couple of chainsaws, axes, handsaws and hefty ropes, they loaded up the vehicles and set off.

Lilly had thrown on a pair of jeans and a sweatshirt. Luckily, she'd found a pair of old walking boots in the back of her car. She was to accompany Walter in his jeep, the interior of which was redolent with fuel from the can in the boot for the chainsaws. Before they'd even travelled for five minutes, she felt a headache coming on and opened the window for much needed fresh air.

"You seem to enjoy your work here, Walter," Lilly said as he pulled out of the immediate property grounds, leading the convoy.

"I do. Very much," he said, concentrating on the road. It was littered with fallen branches and assorted debris, making the journey a slow one. "They are a good family to work for. I'm relatively new compared to the others. I didn't start working here until after Jack got hurt falling from a ladder."

"Yes, you mentioned that," Lilly said. "It sounded traumatic not just for Jack but for the whole family. How bad was it?"

"He hurt his back quite badly, from what I understand. But he also suffered from a head injury of some sort. It was before the Alzheimer's set in. I often wonder if that was the starts of it. It's not my place to ask though. I'm sure the family looked into the possibilities of head trauma. Robert and Sarah and Jack's wife have looked after him well. If I'm honest, I was hoping to see him looking better this time after he started the new treatment, but if anything he seems worse. It's a real shame to see a man with such vigor and vitality as I'm told Jack had, reduced to a mere shell of himself. He was always such good company, apparently."

They remained silent for a while as Walter concentrated on navigating the hazardous road, then Lilly asked Walter just how bad the blockage they were attempting to clear actually was.

"It looked pretty bad last night, but with the rain lashing down and the wind it was difficult to tell. But you're just about to find out. We're here."

They parked on the left of the road, the other two cars stopping behind them. Strewn right across the road were two enormous oak trees, completely wrenched free of the ground, a mass of tangled roots, some as thick as a man, exposed to the air. To the left was the dense wood the trees had once been part of, and to the right the cliff dropping down to the sea below. Lilly could see there was no way any sort of vehicle could drive round them. So armed with the tools they'd brought, the group started to cut the trees into more manageable pieces, which could then be dragged or carried to the verge.

An hour later, hot, sweaty and itching, there wasn't much to show for all their hard work. The trees didn't seem any smaller than they had when they'd arrived. It was going to be a very long job.

"You'd have thought the council would have sent someone up here to clear the road by now," Edward said, swinging an axe.

"We're too far out," Robert said. "I doubt anyone even knows there's a problem up here."

"It could take days for us to clear all this," Fiona said, voicing Lilly's thoughts.

A few more days trapped in a bed-and-breakfast with a murderer was an horrendous thought. There must be a way to get to town and get help, Lilly thought.

"Is it too far to walk into town?" she asked.

"I wouldn't try it," Fiona said. "Who knows what the road ahead looks like? Or the wood for that matter. These trees won't be the only ones to have come down. Besides, you'd end up walking in the dark. It's too dangerous even for those of us who know the area well."

"And we couldn't get a vehicle through those woods?"

"Not on your life," Sarah said, dragging a coil of rope from Walter's jeep. "It's full of massive rocks, gullies and streams. Not to mention the amount of mud there'll be considering the storm."

Lilly realised just how right Sarah was when she stepped into the woodland and sunk up to her ankles. But she was determined to find a way. She wanted to get the police to the house as soon as possible. They were all on edge, with a killer among them. No one felt safe and everyone was leery of the others, which could spill over into something far more serious the longer it went on.

Sleuthing with Chloe had turned up some clues, but they had provided more questions than answers. Freeing her boots from the mire, she decided to go a little deeper into the wood in the hopes the mud would thin out a bit considering the protection of the overhead canopy. She was right, the ground was more solid, but it was still slick and she found herself sliding several times but luckily managed to stay upright by grabbing onto the underbrush. Her immediate goal was to try to get to the other side of the fallen oaks. If they could tackle the obstruction from both sides, it might make the whole job quicker.

She'd not gone too far in when she saw a sight that made her heart skip a beat. In the midst of the trees was an overturned vehicle.

"Robert. Joanne. Everyone!" she shouted, scrambling to get to the car she recognised. "It's Morris, he's in trouble."

❦

LILLY CLAMBERED TO the driver's side of the car, but Morris was nowhere to be seen.

"Oh no, Morris," Dominic cried, first at the scene of the accident.

The rest caught up quickly and with no sign of Morris, began to spread out and shout for him.

"He must have driven straight off the road in the storm and hit that tree," Joanne said, close to tears. "I told him it was too dangerous to go out. He could be lying in the woods somewhere hurt. Or worse. Is there any blood in the car?"

"I don't see any blood," Robert said. "But the windscreen is smashed in, and the driver's side window. We need to find him. He must be lying hurt somewhere after the impact."

Lilly froze. "Maybe not," she said as a sickening thought occurred to her. Everyone turned to face her.

"The dagger," Natalie gasped.

"Did Morris know about the secret passage?" Robert demanded.

"Yes," Dominic said. "All the staff knew about it."

"If Morris made his way back..." Joanne said, unable to finish the sentence.

"Oh my god, Chloe!" Robert cried, spinning on his heel and scrambling back to the road as fast as the conditions would allow.

Everyone else followed, hurrying to their vehicles. Lilly jumped into Walter's jeep as he gunned the engine, spun the car around, and sped up the road just behind Robert and Joanne.

"You don't think Morris killed John, do you?" Walter asked frantically. "He's a nice old man, I just can't imagine him killing someone like that."

Lilly wasn't sure, but the evidence, circumstantial as it was, didn't look good.

"He had a bad altercation with John last night, and it was his dagger we found. You know how loyal he is to Jack, Walter. I don't know either of them, but it's apparent even to me how much Morris cares for Jack. Maybe he thought he was defending him. He said he owed his life to him, remember?"

Walter shook his head in despair as he pulled up in front of The Palms.

"Yes, he and Jack were close, like brothers, in fact," he said, opening the door and jumping out. "But to kill someone over, what? A foul mouth and a bad attitude?"

"Let's not jump to conclusions just yet, Walter. We've no proof it was Morris. We don't even know where he is yet."

Walter nodded, and they both ran inside, just behind the others, listening as Robert called out his daughter's name.

Inside, Lilly was relieved to find Chloe and her granddad sitting at the dining table tucking into sandwiches and fruit juice.

"What's going on?" Chloe asked, eyes wide as everyone charged into the room.

Robert grabbed his daughter and gave her a hug, exhaling with relief.

"Dad, what's happened?"

He let her go and sank into a chair next to her. "It's Morris, Chloe. He crashed his car in the woods not long after he left here last night. We found the car but there's no sign of him."

"Morris," Jack said dreamily. "Where's Morris?"

"I don't know, Dad," Robert said. "He's missing."

The group decided the best thing to do would be split up and search the house, then the outbuildings. Dominic, Edward and Fiona took one half of the ground floor, Walter, Natalie and Sam the other half, while Robert, Joanne and Sarah went upstairs. Lilly was going to join in the search upstairs, but Robert asked if she would stay and keep an eye on Jack and Chloe, a task she was more than happy to do.

While she sat and ate the sandwich Chloe had made for her, Lilly thought about Morris. If he'd staged the accident and doubled back to the house during the night, he could easily have killed John, then disappeared with no one being any the wiser. He knew the house like the back of his hand, having worked there for so long, including the secret passageway. The murder weapon looked to be his, and his argument with John certainly gave him a motive. John was not well liked by anyone, but he had been particularly disparaging towards Morris and had obviously pushed him too far.

The question was, where had he gone?

LILLY HADN'T REALISED how long it had been while her thoughts whirled with the murder until Chloe spoke. She'd been wondering if it really was Morris who was guilty.

"You're not convinced it was Morris who killed John, are you?"

She smiled. The girl was adept at reading her thoughts.

"I'm just worried we're trying to fit the person to what we know rather than having proof. It's dangerous to do that, Chloe. It could ruin lives. We have no evidence to speak of and the facts as we know them could easily fit Natalie as well as Morris. It's all pure conjecture at this point."

"But Morris is missing."

"I know, but he could be hurt and found shelter somewhere. There's nothing to say he came back here at all. The opposite, actually. For one, I've noticed the stairs make quite loud creaking sounds when anyone is on them. Surely someone would have heard them if Morris had come back? Especially in the dead of night when every little noise sounds louder."

"But there was a massive storm outside. Really loud. Maybe it covered it up?"

"Okay. But Natalie was in there with John not long before he was killed. Do you think Morris was really lurking in the shadows, waiting for her to leave? It would take someone a lot braver than me to kill someone in a room while we were all outside the door."

"He could have hidden in the passage."

"Perhaps. But it would have been cutting it extremely fine, considering that was the way Natalie left the room. And what about the mud?"

"What mud?"

"Exactly. I've been down to where his car was crashed, Chloe. The place is like a quagmire. It would have been much worse last night. If Morris sneaked back in, surely there would have been signs of mud and water. Yet there's nothing."

"I suppose," Chloe said, munching her sandwich thoughtfully. "But he could have cleaned up or got changed before he came in. John made him really angry last night with something he said about granddad. They never liked talking about the war. Maybe something happened that John knew about and he brought it up when they were in the kitchen?"

Lilly sighed. "I wonder if anyone else overheard the argument? Morris said it was the derogatory way he spoke about your granddad, but he didn't really go into any detail, did he?"

Chloe shook her head.

There were sounds of footsteps filtering through to the dining room and Lilly realised everyone was gathering in the lounge.

"Give me a minute, Chloe," Lilly said, rising.

"I'll make some more sandwiches. I'm sure everyone will be getting hungry by now."

Lilly nodded. "That's a good idea."

AS LILLY ENTERED the lounge, she could immediately see everyone had broken off into groups. Sarah, Fiona, Dominic and Edward were seated together on the sofa. Robert and Joanne had separated themselves and were in deep discussion in a couple of armchairs. Sam was on his own, seated in front of the fireplace, occasionally jabbing the embers with the poker. And Natalie and Walter were standing in a corner whispering. Lilly felt drawn to them. As staff members, she wondered if their insight and perspective might be different to that of the family.

"Morris wasn't to be found, then?" she asked.

Natalie shook her head.

"I'm wondering if he managed to make it back to town somehow last night," Walter said. "And we're jumping to conclusions."

"Please, Walter," Natalie said. "I've finally got everyone off my back. Let's not give them a reason to start accusing me again."

"You were found in John's room," Lilly said pointedly. "Did you see anything in the passage when you left?"

Natalie's face turned crimson, and she shook her head. "No. But honestly, I was in a rush. That's part of the reason why I had to leave my underwear behind. I didn't have time to look. I was worried about getting caught. When I got back into the hall, I immediately came round the corner to greet all of you. I wanted to make sure I was seen outside the room by Sarah. I knew she didn't know about the passage, and even though I was aware Dominic and Edward knew about it, I was hoping it wouldn't occur to them. I had no choice but to pray they wouldn't bring it up."

"I'm surprised no one at all thought to bring up the secret route to room four," Lilly said, looking at Walter. "What's your excuse, Walter? You could have mentioned it the moment Natalie appeared from that direction, or at least when we found out John was dead. Instead it took Sam, a guest, pointing it out to Chloe and me, while you, Edward and Dominic remained silent. At least Natalie had a genuine reason not to say anything, since she was trying to keep her relationship with John under wraps."

"Yes, well, my job is outside, as you know, Lilly," Walter replied, testily. "I've no reason to be in that part of the house. In all the years I've been here I've used it maybe twice, and that was when I was first shown it. To be honest, I'd forgotten it existed until last night. My first assumption was the same as everyone else's, that Natalie had just been woken up because of all the shouting. I didn't for one minute think she was having an affair with John." He glanced at Natalie as he said this. "I thought better of you, Natalie."

Natalie averted her eyes. "It's not one of my finer moments, and believe me I bitterly regret it now."

"I should think so. Especially with John, of all people. You can do better than that. So could Sarah, truth be told," said Walter.

"No one here seems to think very highly of John," Lilly said. "Except perhaps you, Natalie."

Natalie scowled. "I'm not talking about it anymore. I'll go and make us some lunch."

Lilly was about to tell her Chloe was already doing it when Natalie stormed off in the direction of the kitchen.

"I thought she had more sense than to get involved with the likes of John," Walter sighed, shaking his head.

"You didn't happen to hear any of the argument between Morris and John last night, did you? I know Morris mentioned it was about Jack, but he didn't say much more."

"No, I didn't hear them, but if it involved Jack, I can take a good guess."

"A regular argument?"

Walter nodded. "I'm surprised John hadn't tried harder to convince Sarah and Robert to sack Morris. Usually he got his own way, but they held onto the old man for Jack's sake."

"Why would John be so keen to get rid of Morris?" Lilly asked, intrigued. "Was he a bad cook?"

"No, nothing like that. Quite the opposite, he was a wonderful cook."

"Then why did John want him to leave so badly?"

Walter grew quiet. Then taking her arm pulled her as far away from the group as he could and lowered his voice.

"Listen, I don't know for sure what happened the day Jack fell from the ladder, but Morris... well... he had his suspicions."

Lilly felt a cold shiver down her back.

"Go on. What do you know, Walter?"

"I wasn't working here at the time, but Morris once told me in confidence he was convinced John had deliberately pushed Jack off that ladder."

Chapter Nine

"WHAT?" LILLY SAID, shocked. "Are you sure, Walter?"

"John, Morris and Jack were the only ones there that day, from what I understand," Walter said. "Jack was at the top of the ladder working on the guttering. John was standing on the roof itself, replacing broken tiles, and Morris told me he and John were having some sort of argument. The next thing Morris knew, Jack was on the ground. He didn't actually see it happen, but sort of sensed it, so he told me. He'd turned and saw Jack hit the ground, saw an instant look of satisfaction on John's face when he glanced up. But it was only for a split second. He didn't actually see John push Jack, so couldn't prove it. Jack hit his head hard and was rushed to hospital. When he regained consciousness, he couldn't remember anything at all about what had happened."

"What about you, Walter? Do you think John was capable of pushing his father-in-law off a ladder from that height? He could have killed him."

Walter shrugged. "I'm not committing one way or the other. But I will say we're all better off without John in our lives. He treated all of us dreadfully, especially poor Sarah. She's in shock and upset now, but she'll come round and see him for the abuser he was in time. I can't believe Robert put up with him for so long. If he'd been married to my sister, I would have dealt with him a long time ago."

"Walter..."

He held his hands up in defense. "I didn't do anything, it's not my place. Nor do I think it would be the right thing to do. All I'm saying is John seriously mistreated Sarah and if she wouldn't or couldn't do anything about it... well, maybe Robert should have."

Lilly sighed. This was becoming more and more complicated, but she understood Walter's sentiments. As a former agony aunt she'd received letters from abused spouses and knew the long term emotional, mental and physical damage it caused.

"Walter, John is dead, so whether he pushed Jack or not is a moot point now. Can't you tell me in confidence what you think? Did John really push Jack?"

"No, I can't, but Morris certainly thought so, and he loves Jack. He's been holding onto pent-up rage over the incident for years. Maybe it just came to a head this weekend? It doesn't really matter whether John pushed Jack, what matters is that Morris believed he did. And with Jack out of the way, Robert and Sarah would get this place. Which ultimately they did."

"You think that's what it was about?"

"It wouldn't surprise me. You know, John was the one who originally hired me and that's been a problem. He's been holding it over my head from day one, subtly threatening me whenever he got the chance. Letting me know he could sack me at any time. It was a power thing with him. I think that's why he sacked Edward. He wanted the staff to know that if he could get rid of a member of Joanne's family, when she's married to one of the owners, then he could do it to any of us."

"You certainly paint an appalling picture of him, Walter."

"That's how he was. I miss the days when he only came up occasionally. I could stay out of the way then. It wasn't until Joanne came on board that he suddenly wanted to be involved with the business. He didn't like the idea of a new in-law, especially a woman, having more say than he did. He felt threatened by her and was worried she would voice what Robert should have been saying all along."

"Which was?"

"That Sarah should leave him. He hated his wife having supportive girlfriends and wanted to make sure he knew what Joanne was saying to Sarah about him. When Sarah and Fiona became friends, it began to get a lot worse. I think that's another reason why he fired Edward, to stir tension within the family and stop Sarah from getting too close to anyone. Fiona's not visited as much since then."

Lilly nodded. "I agree with you, Walter. I've seen it before where an abuser and a bully manipulates the situation, essentially to isolate the victim, meaning the only one they can turn to is the abuser."

"And that's why we're all better off without him, Lilly."

FTER LUNCH, LILLY volunteered to help Chloe with the washing up. She could tell Chloe had something on her mind and wanted to talk to her about what she'd learned herself from Walter.

With no power the dishwasher wasn't working, so they boiled pans of water on the hob, filled the sink and did it by hand.

Lilly embraced the job of doing something normal and mundane like washing dishes. It took her mind off what had happened and the tense atmosphere when the family were all in the same room together.

As she scrubbed and rinsed, she wondered about Robert and Joanne. Were two people she had known for five years and considered good friends capable of murder? She hated the thought and in her heart didn't believe it to be true, but she couldn't dismiss them as suspects. She let her mind wander, thinking through what they knew so far.

The fact there was a secret passage that no one had bothered to mention struck her as odd. Could those who knew about it be protecting someone? All those who knew the secret had despised the victim, but enough to kill him, Lilly couldn't be sure. There just weren't enough clues to point to one person. Morris certainly stood out in her mind, but there was no indication that he'd come back to the house that night. In fact, the absence of any traces suggested the complete opposite.

Chloe took a plate from the stack on the draining board, dried it, then put it back in the sink. Lilly glanced at her. She was in a daze.

"I've just washed that one. What's on your mind, Watson?" Lilly said.

"Oh, sorry. I'm just thinking about suspects."

Lilly chuckled. "I thought you might be. Want to tell me what you're thinking?"

She appreciated Chloe's thoughts. She had insider information she, herself, wouldn't be able to get from the family or the employees, and she was observant. Perhaps Chloe had some answers that she wasn't aware of, which could help Lilly sort out her own suspicions. "Let me make us some ginger and honey tea. It helps with brain function and mine is feeling very fuzzy at the moment."

"I think the most obvious suspect is Morris," Chloe said, putting down the tea towel and leaning against the counter. "He's missing. He argued with John only a few hours before he was murdered. And, he definitely blames John for what happened to granddad. I heard him talking to Walter ages ago about it. He knew about the secret passage and it was his dagger that was used. It all points to Morris, doesn't it?"

"It certainly looks that way, but I can tell you have other ideas."

"Yeah, I do," Chloe admitted. "I can't believe Morris could have got in without any of us hearing or seeing him. Especially as Natalie claims to have been in the room with John not ten minutes before we all came in and said he was still alive then."

"So, you think Natalie is the guilty party?"

"I think it's more likely than Morris," Chloe said. "But what's her motive? She doesn't have one, not really. The one with the most motive is Aunt Sarah. She thought her husband was having an affair, and she was right. Plus, John treated her really badly. I'll never let any man treat me like that. But I don't know how she could have done it and then been in the hall without Natalie seeing her. Unless they are working together. But that doesn't seem likely. Aunt Sarah doesn't like Natalie, especially now."

"It's good to brainstorm like this, Chloe. It helps you see things more clearly and work out what is possible and what's not. I'd have to say it's almost impossible for your aunt to be guilty. There wouldn't have been enough time."

Chloe nodded. "Yes, you're right. Now I think about it. The only one I can say was there the whole time was Aunt Sarah. And she didn't know about the secret door as far as we know. But there was a lot of commotion in the hall. Anyone could have slipped in and out then joined us. I can't say with certainty that any of the others were there the whole time, though. And let's be honest, just about everyone has a motive. Well, except dad and Joanne. They didn't like John but I know they didn't kill him."

Lilly nodded, she'd come to the same conclusion herself but she wasn't about to upset Chloe by explaining neither Robert nor Joanne could be eliminated from the suspect list just yet. Placing the tea on the kitchen table, she sat and Chloe joined her. "Walter said John held his job over his head often. He wasn't pleased about it."

"And Dominic and Edward totally hated him," Chloe said. "Ever since he sacked Edward, the two of them have had nothing but bad things to say about him. Same for Fiona. She always felt her sons were targeted by John because he never felt Joanne was part of the family, and therefore neither were Fiona, Dominic or Edward. And I know Fiona's been trying to talk Sarah into leaving John for years."

"You haven't mentioned that before," Lilly said. "Although when I spoke to Walter earlier, he suggested the same thing; that he was intimidated by Joanne and Fiona because he didn't want his wife having friends who would try to persuade her to see what her husband was really like."

"Fiona said he was abusive and I think she's right. Aunt Sarah always had a few bruises, from being clumsy and walking into stuff, she said. But I already guessed that wasn't true."

"Do you think Fiona might have killed John to protect Sarah?" Lilly asked.

Chloe shrugged, staring into her tea. "I don't know. Maybe. It's really hard wondering if someone in your family is a murderer."

"Chloe, we can stop this at any time. I don't want you upset. We should let the police deal with it."

"We can't wait that long. And I need to do something otherwise my family will all fall out and then what will happen?"

Lilly didn't have answers for her, but she knew Chloe was right. The arguments and the animosity among the family were barely below surface level now, and sooner or later words would be spoken that could never be taken back. She didn't want this family, who obviously loved each other dearly, to become estranged, with no chance of healing or making amends in the future.

And then there was Sam. He wasn't family, but he knew a lot more about the place than the owners. Just who exactly was he?

◊◊◊

*L*ILLY AND CHLOE walked back into the lounge just as Robert announced his plan to go and search for Morris. Hearing this, Lilly volunteered to go with him. Whether he was the murderer or not, it was suspicious enough that he was missing. He needed to be found in order to be able to give his side of the story, one way or another. Assuming he wasn't lying injured or dead somewhere.

Chloe had naturally wanted to go with them, but Robert put his foot down. He wanted her safe in the bed-and-breakfast with the others, in particular her stepmother Joanne.

"I think you have a fan in my daughter, Lilly," Robert said as they left the building.

"She's a lovely girl, Robert. You should be very proud. She's also very astute and observant."

"She's been helping you investigate, hasn't she? She read the articles in the Plumpton Mallet Gazette and since then she's devoured Sherlock Holmes and Agatha Christie. She wants to be just like you. It's worrying me if I'm honest. She wasn't close to John and consequently I feel she's treating this more like a game. But it's real, and the fact is someone she knows and is probably close to, heaven forbid it's a family member, has committed murder. I'm terrified of what it will do to her when we discover who it was."

"It was my first thought, Robert. I've talked to her about it and I'm keeping a close eye on her. I promise if it gets too much for her I'll stop it. But at the moment she's frightened her family is going to fall out permanently, that's why she wants so desperately to find out who did it."

"Yes, I can understand that. It's got me concerned too, actually. Apart from John the whole family has always got on well with each other, but now we're constantly bickering and falling out. Not to mentioned blaming one another for what's happened. It's stressful and is ripping the family apart, Lilly. The trust is all but gone, and I don't want it to get to the stage where it can't ever be resolved. We need to find out who is responsible as soon as possible if the police can't get here to help us. Would you mind continuing to see what you can find out?

"Yes, of course I will, Robert."

"Thank you. And thank you for keeping an eye on Chloe too. Now, I think we should start looking in the outbuildings for Morris."

There weren't many external buildings to check; a couple of sheds, one Walter's domain, the other used for storage, and both were small with no sign of Morris. The other was a larger barn, which they tackled last.

They stepped inside and looked around the dim interior. There was some entertainment equipment on the ground floor which had been used for the party, along with old bits of furniture in need of repair, probably from the main house, Lilly thought, but not much else. Robert took the stairs up to the loft and Lilly followed, but there was no sign of Morris, nor any trace that anyone had been up here in a long time.

"Well, he's not been here," Robert said as they stepped back outside.

As Lilly turned, she spotted a lone figure walking down the path in the direction of the orchard.

"Who is that?"

Robert squinted his eyes and shook his head. "I don't know. Come on."

They hurried towards the figure, both of them half expecting Morris to turn round. Instead, as they drew closer, Lilly realised it was Sam outside by himself, hands in his pockets as though taking a casual stroll.

"Sam. What are you doing out here? I told everyone to stay inside, safe and together."

"I needed some fresh air. It's getting stuffy inside. Besides, I wanted to talk to you, Robert. I just remembered something from my childhood visits that may help locate Morris."

Lilly and Robert exchanged glances. Sam grinned and beckoned them forward. "Follow me," he said, continuing down the path.

"Where are we going, Sam?" Lilly asked, all too aware this man was as much a suspect as everyone else.

"I told you this place holds a lot of secrets."

"What do you mean, Sam," Robert asked. "Is there something else I don't know about?"

"I don't know what you know and what you don't, Robert. It is your business, after all. But I wondered how much exploration you've done of this place? Do you know about the old clubhouse?"

Lilly glanced at Robert. He looked totally confused.

"What? What clubhouse?"

"There's an old abandoned clubhouse not too far from where Morris's car was found," Sam said. "I'd forgotten all about it until I was just chatting with Chloe and reminiscing about exploring when I was a boy. Mind you, it was nearly thirty years ago so could very well be gone now."

"You didn't know about it, Robert?" Lilly asked.

Robert shook his head. "No. I've never heard about it until now."

"And you think Morris could be hiding in there, Sam?" Lilly asked.

"Well, he doesn't seem to be anywhere else, unless he managed to get to town, but I doubt he would have made it in the storm. No, if the place is still standing then I think there's a good chance he's taken shelter in there."

Once more they followed Sam, but Lilly felt uneasy. There was just something about him that was off. He knew far more about The Palms than even the owners did. First the secret doors and the passage, now a long abandoned clubhouse. It was too much. Why was he even here this weekend? Was it actually an accidental booking, like he'd said?

They walked for at least half an hour before Sam veered off into the thick woodland. A few yards away Lilly caught a glimpse of Morris's car, but the route Sam took them continued deeper into the trees and soon she lost sight of the car and the road altogether.

"We still need to move the trees in the road," she said to Robert to break the unnerving silence.

"I know. But I'd like to find Morris first."

Tiffin & Tragedy

Sam led them further through the woods, and Lilly began to feel more nervous with every step. Was there really a clubhouse this way, or was Sam taking them to a secluded spot to get rid of them? She hadn't noticed him carrying a weapon of any sort, but it could be cleverly concealed. She and Robert could possibly win in a fair fight, but against a weapon they would have no chance. Just as she was about to stop and turn round, she spotted the moss covered roof of a small wooden structure in the distance. Covered in brambles and surrounded by stinging nettles, it was so well camouflaged it was barely noticeable unless you were looking for it.

"You were telling the truth," Lilly said.

"You sound surprised," Sam said. "Why would I make up the existence of an old clubhouse?"

To get us in the middle of nowhere and bump us off, Lilly thought. But kept quiet.

"Right," Robert said. "Let's see if Morris is in there, shall we? I have questions for him."

IT WAS A modest size structure that had definitely seen better days. Thrown together with old wooden panels, most likely off-cuts from the time when the bed-and-breakfast or the barn was built. There was a square cut out in the side that once would have been a window. Now, no glass remained, and it was open to the elements. Lilly was amazed it was still standing.

Sam held out his arm. "After you, Robert."

Robert nodded, and took a step forward, but Lilly decided to stay just behind Sam in case he tried something.

The wooden door creaked a little as Robert pushed it open, but surprisingly, it moved quite smoothly on its rusty hinges. Lilly had expected it to fall in.

As they entered and their eyes adjusted to the internal gloom, they all saw the figure of Morris sprawled out on top of an old mattress in the corner, covered in an old tarpaulin and snoring loudly. An old empty whiskey bottle at his side.

Robert kicked the bottom of Morris's boot and the old man groaned.

"Morris, wake up!" Robert shouted.

Morris came to slowly, groaning and rubbing his eyes until he could focus.

"Robert? What are you doing here? What time is it?"

"It's two in the afternoon. What are you doing here?"

Morris slowly shifted to a sitting position, clutching his head, and Lilly could see a bump the size of a small egg on his temple just beginning to bruise.

"Crashed my car in the storm last night. I tried to make it back but lost all sense of direction. Then I remembered this place. Got soaked but at least it kept me out of the rain."

"Morris," Lilly said. "How do you feel? You've hit your head and could have a concussion. Drinking whiskey was a stupid idea after crashing your car."

Morris looked sheepishly at Lilly. "Yes, I expect you're right. I found an unopened bottle in here and couldn't resist. I obviously overdid it. Too late now, though. At least I woke up, although my head hurts."

"Get up, Morris. You need to get back to the house and get some warm clothes on, you've slept all night in wet gear," Robert said, hoisting the old man up by his arm and steadying him while he swayed a little. Once he was stable, they exited the clubhouse and began the slow journey back to The Palms.

Before she left, Lilly had checked inside the ramshackle shed for clues but had seen nothing. There was also no blood on Morris's clothes, but he'd had plenty of time to change them. Unlikely, but possible. However, if Morris did kill John, he was probably no danger to them now, hungover and exhausted as he was, he could barely put one foot in front of the other without help.

Once again Sam led the way with Morris next and Robert just behind him, ostensibly within easy reach should the old man stumble. But, Lilly could tell Robert no longer trusted Morris and had positioned himself in such a way so he could intervene should he suddenly take it into his head to attack or to make a run for it. Lilly brought up the rear, glad they were returning with Morris in tow. Maybe now they'd all get some answers.

Chapter Ten

*I*N AN ATTEMPT to sober Morris up and get rid of his hangover, Lilly offered to make him one of her special teas. However, Morris said he didn't hold with any of the newfangled stuff and preferred strong hot coffee. Lilly would have laughed if the situation weren't so serious. Tea had been around for hundreds of years.

Boiling a pan of water on the hob as the power was still off, she filled a small cafetière with the strongest grounds she could find. With the coffee tray complete, she took it to the empty lounge to wait. Robert had taken Morris back to his room to get washed and changed. He wasn't taking any chances that Morris would disappear again. Lilly hoped a cleaner and more sober Morris would return. Everybody else had dispersed, but she expected them all back once Morris made an appearance.

They began to turn up in ones and twos; Dominic threw a couple of logs on the fire, then took a seat, waiting in silence. By the time they were all gathered, with Morris sitting as close to the fire as he could and sipping the coffee Lilly had made, the questions began.

"Morris, what on earth happened last night?" Joanne said.

"I've already told Robert. I crashed the car in the storm. It was so dark out there I lost all sense of direction and went off course in the woods. Then I came across the old clubhouse and decided to take shelter until the storm blew itself out. I must have fallen asleep."

"A clubhouse I didn't even know existed, and I expect the whiskey helped put you to sleep," Robert said.

Morris shrugged. "I had to keep warm somehow. It worked."

"So you never came back here at all last night?"

"No. I've just said I got disoriented and ended up exactly where you found me, Robert. I apologise for my temper and my conduct last night, but John was out of order. I've never been so angry. Speaking of John, where is he? Not being his usual lazy self and still in bed is he? I'd have thought he'd have been here relishing the chance to tear a strip off me."

Sarah suddenly burst into tears and promptly rushed from the room. Morris, wide eyed, watched her leave.

"I didn't mean to upset her. What did I say? Did her and John have another argument after I left? If he hurt her, I swear..."

"John's dead," Fiona said, cutting Morris off before he could make things worse. "Somebody killed him."

Morris smirked, then glancing around at the sea of serious faces, realised this was no joke.

"What? Dear god, I didn't know. What happened?"

"John was stabbed in his sleep last night," Walter said.

Robert let out a huge sigh. "I'm going to check on Sarah. Morris, be careful what you say in front of her. She's in a delicate state at the moment," he said, hurrying after his distraught sister.

Morris looked at Joanne, understanding and sympathy etched on his face. "I didn't know, Joanne. I didn't mean to upset Sarah. I didn't know what had happened."

Joanne nodded. "I can see you didn't, Morris."

Lilly had been watching Morris intently while the conversation was taking place and she could see he was both sorry he had offended Sarah and seemingly genuinely shocked John was dead. But if he wasn't the one to kill John, then they were back to square one as far as suspects were concerned. Lilly waited to see what the family would ask next, keeping her thoughts to herself for the time being.

"Wait a minute, Aunt Joanne," Edward said. "Just because Morris was found in the clubhouse this morning doesn't mean he didn't sneak back here last night. It was his army knife that was the murder weapon."

Morris's eyes widened as the realisation dawned on him. "Hang on a minute! You don't all think I did this, do you? I wasn't even here."

"But you and John had a massive row last night," Dominic said.

"Yes, but I left," Morris shouted. "I didn't even know he was dead until you just told me."

TIFFIN & TRAGEDY

"But we only have your word for that," Edward said. "It's not like you're going to admit it, is it? You could easily have sneaked back here. It makes sense doesn't it?" He asked the others. "We were all in the hallway when it happened, but where was Morris? We don't know for sure he left the property like he said. He could have pretended to drive off, parked the car out of sight and come back and murdered John. Then really left and made his way to the clubhouse after he crashed his car. I didn't even know the clubhouse was there, and neither did Robert from what he just said. It's very convenient Morris knew about it."

Immediately, the room erupted into an argument. With accusations flying and Morris vehemently protesting his innocence, Lilly, not wanting to get dragged into yet another family argument, slipped away unnoticed. She did, however, remain outside the door, listening to the drama unfold.

Both Dominic and Edward were convinced Morris had initially left the house and then returned to kill John. He had both the time and the motive. Joanne tentatively agreed to the possibility her nephews posed, but Morris fiercely objected, pointing out he was not the only one with a motive. He reminded Edward that John had sacked him and Dominic that he, too, had argued with John that day. Dominic disagreed, saying it was nothing more than a minor squabble. No more serious than any of the others they'd had in the past.

"And it didn't end up with John being covered in hot soup," he finished.

"After what he said about Robert's father, a soaking in soup was the least he deserved," Morris said.

The room grew quiet, and Lilly moved closer to the door.

"The least he deserved?" Edward repeated.

"Oh, for crying out loud, Edward. Stop putting words in my mouth. I didn't mean it like that. Surely you all know me well enough to recognise I would never kill anyone."

"What about in the army? You've obviously got skills and experience," Dominic said quietly.

"That's no one's business but my own."

"Dominic, that's enough," Joanne said. "Although," she said, turning to Morris, "It does add more fuel to the flames."

"Oh, Joanne," Morris said sadly. "I don't know what I can say to make you believe me. It's true, I didn't like John. He was not a good person. But can anyone here say, in all honesty, that they liked him? He was bad to the core, you all know that. A bully, a thug, and he had a vicious mouth. He was cruel to Jack and to Sarah, and treated everyone else like they were his personal servants. But I did not kill him. Why would I risk going to prison for someone like that?"

There was a lull in the conversation after Morris had finished speaking, and Lilly moved away to think more about the possibilities. She thought about the knife she and Chloe had found. If Morris had found out John was having an affair with Natalie, it could have been the final straw. He was already furious at the way John treated Jack, but what would he do if he found out his best friend's daughter was married to an adulterer? Perhaps this was what had driven him to kill John? If indeed it was Morris. Lilly realised she needed more evidence to back up her thoughts and wondered where she should search to find it?

Then it occurred to her that while she and Chloe had searched room four thoroughly, they had forgotten to examine the secret passage. Perhaps the perpetrator had left some sort of evidence behind that could point them in the right direction?

She headed upstairs, eager to try to piece this mystery together once and for all.

As LILLY REACHED the top of the stairs, she heard a creak behind her and spun round to see Chloe following her.

"What are you doing here?" she whispered.

"I know you're on the case again," she whispered back. "I want to help. I'm your Watson remember?"

"Fine, just keep your voice down, okay?"

Chloe scurried over, looking excited. "So what's your plan? Are you going to search some of the other staff rooms? I know we found some evidence in Natalie's room, but maybe there's something we missed? What about Morris's room? He looks really suspicious, doesn't he? We should probably search his room too and see if there's anything in there."

"Chloe, take a breath, would you? You're making me dizzy," Lilly said, amused. "Actually, I was going to take a look in that secret passage. We missed it last time."

"Good idea. Although it's not very long, what could we possibly find in there?"

"Probably nothing, but you never know. It needs checking either way."

They arrived at the bookshelf in the hallway and pulled it open. Lilly leading the way with the torch lit on her phone. As she moved down the short hall, the light caught the wall and Chloe grabbed her shoulder.

"What's that?"

Lilly took a closer look. "They're signatures. See the dates, Chloe? These go back to the time The Palms was built. I don't recognise any of the early ones, but look here, there's Sam's name. He must have written that when he was a child judging by the immature scrawl."

"He has been coming here a long time, like he said. Look here! That's Granddad's name. I think it was the year after he bought the place."

"And these are Dominic and Edward's signatures. That's when they first started working here, is it?" Lilly said, looking at the date.

"Yes," Chloe said, running her hand along the names. "Here's Natalie, and Morris and this one is Walter."

"This is consistent with what everyone's told us so far. I'm not sure there's anything to find in here, Chloe."

She started to turn to leave the passage when she kicked something. Looking down, she saw an object, small and metallic skitter across the floor.

"What was that?" Chloe asked, having heard the same sound.

Lilly crouched and picked up the coin sized object, turning it over.

"It's a military medal. The words say *For Bravery in the Field*. It's usually given to soldiers who sustained injury during battle."

"Morris," Chloe said, shaking her head. "I honestly was hoping we'd find the evidence we needed against Natalie. I don't like the idea of it being Morris, I like him. He's an old family friend and I don't want him to go to prison."

"I know, Chloe. But if he killed John, then it's what will happen, I'm afraid. You know there's not a speck of dust on this medal, that would suggest it was dropped recently."

"Like last night. Looks like we've solved it, doesn't it?"

"Not yet," Lilly said, tucking the medal in her pocket. "I think it's time we searched the other rooms."

Chloe nodded. "Okay."

"I THINK WE SHOULD start with Sam's room," Chloe said once they were back in the hall.

"Why his room?"

"It's elementary," she said with a grin.

Lilly laughed. "Very good. Go on, Watson, dazzle me with your thought process."

"Because he knows too much and I think he's up to something."

Not exactly a scientific hypothesis worthy of Sherlock, but it was to the point and Lilly had come to the same conclusion. It was interesting to see Chloe arrive at the same assumption. However, she did wonder if there was more to it.

"Are you sure you're not just worried about what we might find if we start looking in your family's rooms?" she asked gently.

Chloe nodded. "Yes, I am. It scares me to think any of my family did this, Lilly. I was hoping we could do the staff and guest rooms first then if we don't find anything... you know, we'll have to search their suites. Is that okay?"

Lilly gave the girl a quick hug. "Yes, of course it's okay. And for what it's worth I think you're right about looking into Sam first. But you'll need to stay and keep watch in the corridor for me, okay?"

The girl nodded, and the two of them approached Sam's room. Once again, Chloe produced the master key from her pocket and gave it to Lilly. She carefully opened the door and entered quietly. The room was in semidarkness with the lights off and the voiles drawn across the windows, but Lilly could immediately see there was a table under the window which had been set up with a laptop computer. She reached it in three long strides and opened it but was unable to access anything, as it needed a password. To the side was a spiral-bound notebook filled with pages of notes. It was a detailed description of Robert and Joanne's time at the bed-and-breakfast going back several months.

Lilly was flabbergasted. "What on earth? She muttered, turning pages to discover Sam had not only been following her friends around the business, but on all their trips to town and elsewhere. *Why has he been following them?* Lilly wondered, taking her phone and photographing the pages. *He's been following Chloe, too! What is all this?*

She replaced the notebook and began opening the drawers. At the bottom of the right one she found an official looking manila envelope. Opening it, she discovered what looked like a contract and at the top was John's name. Before she could read further to discover what it was for, someone cleared their throat.

Lilly let out a surprised yell, and spun round to find Sam sitting in a corner, apparently having been there the entire time, watching her search through his private belongings.

"Sam!"

Sam grinned at her. "You are a very nosy person, Lilly Tweed. Although not very observant it must be said, considering you failed to notice me reading in the corner."

Having heard Lilly's shout, Chloe came bursting into the room, also startled at seeing Sam casually sitting inside the room.

"When did you come up here?" Lilly asked. "I swore you were in the lounge when I left."

"When you two were rummaging around in the passage. The constant bickering downstairs was giving me a headache, so I thought I'd come up here and read for a while. Then you came in. I nearly let on I was here but was intrigued as to what you'd come for."

"And I found it," Lilly said, snatching the notebook from the table and holding it up. "Just what is this, Sam? You've been stalking Robert, Joanne and Chloe. Making notes of their every move for the last several months. I think you'd better explain yourself."

"What?" Chloe said, snatching the journal from Lilly's hand and reading it for herself. "You've been spying on us? Why?"

"Spying, stalking. It all sounds so seedy and vulgar doesn't it? I prefer another term." He got up and started towards them.

Lilly instinctively tensed and held her arm in front of Chloe for protection. But Sam merely held out his hand for the envelope she was still holding. Reluctantly, Lilly passed it over.

"This," Sam began. "Is a contract. Several months ago John hired me to dig up some dirt on Robert and Joanne."

Chloe blinked. "What? What do you mean?"

"I'm a detective, Chloe. A private investigator, actually. About a year or so ago, during one of my visits, John and I got talking and when he found out what I did for a living, he hired me on the spot. Told me he wanted something on his brother-in-law."

"But why?"

"For leverage, apparently. As you know your father and aunt are the ones who legally own The Palms, Joanne and John just help out their spouses but have no legal claim on anything. It's deliberately and legally written in that way so if there's ever a divorce or a separation the business would remain in the family. Now, your step mother is perfectly fine with that. She and Robert have an excellent marriage and relationship. John, on the other hand, wanted more. Much more. He wanted control of the business and eventually to buy Robert out. Unfortunately for John, Robert had no intention of selling. He knew John was abusing Sarah, and he's been trying to persuade her to leave him for years."

"But John was worried that if Sarah began to listen and see him for what he really was, he risked losing everything. If they divorced he wouldn't get anything, especially if the abuse was proved. So he hired you to find something he could blackmail Robert and Joanne with?" Lilly said, immediately grasping the situation.

"Exactly that. Robert and Sarah, then latterly Joanne, put in a huge amount of work to get this place back on its feet. John wanted to take it from them."

"And you were going to help him do it, by investigating my family." Chloe said, seething.

"It's no different from what you're doing except it's my job and I get paid."

"But I'm not investigating my dad and step mum."

"You can't have it both ways, Chloe. Investigate someone you don't like in the hopes of finding incriminating evidence, but choose not to pursue someone you do like, purely because they're family or you think they are nice. Many seemingly nice people commit crimes too, you know, and they are all part of someone's family. But rest assured I don't have a horse in this race, Chloe," Sam said.

"And what's that supposed to mean?"

"It means," said Lilly. "He doesn't have a vested interest one way or another. He simply wants to get to the truth by doing the job he's been hired to do."

"Exactly. But if it's any consolation, Chloe, I had no idea what sort of man John was. He was always very friendly, polite and solicitous to guests."

"Because they pay."

"Of course. If there was one thing a man like John appreciated, it was money. Especially if he didn't have to earn it himself. But as I told him, there simply wasn't any dirt to dig up. I've followed them for months and as I know this place inside out it was easy. All I discovered is that they are good people. John still owed me money, two payments on the original price. He's the one who booked me in this weekend, actually, not Sarah. He'd tried to negotiate a lower fee, as I didn't find anything he could use. That's not the way it works of course."

"I knew Aunt Sarah wouldn't have made that sort of mistake. So John brought you here on purpose this weekend?"

Sam nodded. "He was hoping with all the family being present I'd be able to find something. One last attempt to dig up something he could blackmail them over. But then he was killed, and I had to change tactics. I've been trying to find out who is responsible ever since."

"So, you're an actual detective?" Chloe asked.

"A private investigator," Sam corrected.

"What have you found out, Sam?" Lilly asked. "Are you near to discovering who killed John?"

Sam smiled and shook his head. "Not yet, but I think I'm getting close. You see, I was up for most of the night John was murdered. I suffer from bouts of insomnia, particularly when I'm on a job. I may have a bit of intelligence for you amateur detectives."

"Well, tell us what you know," Lilly said.

Sam walked to the desk, picked up a pen, and took his notebook back from Chloe.

"Oh, no. You share first and then maybe we can work out together who killed John."

Chapter Eleven

JUST AS LILLY was beginning to feel she and Chloe had hit the detective jackpot by discovering a real private investigator to help them, Sam started bouncing in the hallway like he was on springs, almost ruining his credibility.

"You see," he said, pacing back and forth. He stepped in the middle of the floor and there was an audible creaking noise. "There's a loose floorboard."

"Okay," Lilly and Chloe said simultaneously.

"I told you I couldn't sleep. The loose floorboard at the end of the hall is unavoidable. In fact, all three of these boards creak."

As he explained, Sam proceeded to step back and forth making each board groan loudly in turn to make sure they understood.

"Now, my room is just there," he said, pointing to the door they'd all just exited. "If someone was attempting to get into the passage connected to room four, they absolutely would have stepped on these boards causing them to creak."

"So, are you saying you didn't hear anyone?" Lilly asked, not entirely sure what Sam was getting at.

"On the contrary, I distinctly remember hearing this sound shortly after Sarah began banging on the door for her husband. Presumably, it was Natalie Sampson sneaking away from the room just as you all started gathering outside the door. But, and this is the interesting part, I then heard it a second time as the rest of you congregated around Sarah. In other words, someone entered the passage while you were all otherwise engaged further up the hall."

Chloe frowned. "You think a creaking floorboard is enough to prove Natalie's innocence?" she asked. "She could have re-entered the room along the passage, standing on the loose floorboard just as easily as someone else could."

"Perhaps," Sam said. Then pointed down the hallway. "But everyone else's rooms are in that direction. They would have come from over there. It wouldn't have made sense for anyone to be in this part of the hall apart from Natalie, who was attempting to sneak away in order to come up behind everyone looking as though she'd just woken up. Besides, if Natalie's intention was to kill John, why not do it the first time? She was already in the room."

"So, let me get this straight," Lilly said. "You heard the floorboard creak after Natalie had left the passageway, but before we'd all managed to get into room four?"

"I heard three actually, but I've ascertained one was Robert going downstairs for the master key then returning, so we can eliminate those. Natalie had already left the passage, then she joined everyone in the hall. Robert went for the key and returned. It was at that point someone else entered the passage, while you were all outside room four."

"And that's when we're all assuming John was stabbed, while we were outside the door," Lilly said. "Unless it was Natalie who stabbed him."

"But Sam says he heard someone else enter the passage after Natalie left," Chloe said. "The only person who could have done that without being noticed by at least *someone* in the hallway was Morris, because we all thought he'd left."

"So where was the killer when we all charged into the room?" Lilly asked.

"Still in the passage," Sam said.

"You honestly believe the killer had the audacity to remain in the passage while we were all in the room discovering John's body?" Lilly asked.

"I'm almost sure of it," Sam said. "I should have pointed out the secret entrance there and then, and I suspect we'd have caught the killer literally red-handed. Too worried to leave and run the risk of being caught."

"Well, why didn't you?" Chloe demanded.

"Because, quite frankly, I was shocked at finding my client dead. The only thing I could think of was that someone had worked out that John had hired me, and if that was the case, then there was a good chance I would be next. I played the scenarios over and over in my mind while I was in that room and came to the conclusion my best approach was to remain quiet and investigate to see if I could unveil the killer myself before he or she got to me. I didn't put two and two together about the creaking floorboards and the passage until later."

"If you really believe the killer was in the passage while we were all in the room, it really only leaves one person who could have done this," Lilly said.

Chloe's shoulders slumped. "Morris," she said sadly.

Sam nodded. "Yes. I'm sorry, but it does appear that way."

SAM MADE HIS way back downstairs, leaving Lilly and Chloe alone. No matter how straightforward Sam's information and conclusion was, for some reason Lilly was still having doubts.

"I feel we still don't have enough to prove Morris is guilty, Chloe. If he really did kill John, then it makes absolutely no sense for him to be found on the property, even if it was quite far away. He wouldn't have sheltered in an old shed then drunk himself to sleep no matter how bad the storm, he would have taken the risk and kept running, getting as much distance between the scene of the crime and himself as possible."

Chloe was stunned, and stared at Lilly for a second before speaking. "Are you serious? All the clues point to him. It was his knife that was the murder weapon; we found his medal in the secret passage. He argued with John and then left giving himself a sort of alibi. But he could have easily come back."

"I know all that, Chloe, but what does it prove? We thought it was Natalie to start with."

"Well, surely we can't get it wrong twice?"

"I expect it's more common than you think. Look, I know it doesn't look good for Morris but we haven't actually investigated anyone else yet have we? Morris and Natalie aside, there are plenty of other people here and none of them liked John," Lilly said. "I just want to make sure we eliminate all other options before we jump to any conclusions. It's a man's life we're talking about, Chloe. We can't afford to make any mistakes."

"Okay," Chloe sighed. "What do you think we should do?"
"Finish snooping."
"All right. Let's get on with it."

They began to go through every room meticulously, but didn't find anything that could be considered interesting as far as the crime was concerned. In her granddad's room, Chloe found his Alzheimer's medication and a love note from his wife which apparently he kept by his side. It was very loving and sentimental, and both Chloe and Lilly were saddened by the fact he'd probably never be able to read it. Even if somebody else volunteered to read it for him, it was unlikely he would be able to concentrate long enough to understand the content. But it was a wonderfully romantic gesture and was obvious the two of them had been very much in love. Lilly took photos just to be thorough.

Nothing even remotely suspicious was found in Robert and Joanne's room, nor in what was now just Sarah's, though Lilly did learn Joanne had a bird watching hobby. There were several books on the subject next to the window, alongside a pair of binoculars. Lilly imagined on most days, when a violent storm hadn't just happened, there would be numerous garden and sea birds to watch outside.

Dominic's room was the smallest but yielded nothing of value except an interesting collection of action figures. Fiona and Edward's guest rooms drew a blank, as did Walter's.

They did, however, find something significant in Morris's room, which didn't help his situation at all. A matching knife to the one used as the murder weapon, suggesting he had a set. The drawer to his desk where they found it had been left partially open; signifying he'd probably grabbed one quickly and had failed to close it properly.

"Satisfied?" Chloe asked as they left the last of the rooms, having taken a picture of the army knife found in Morris's drawer.

"I suppose so. We've cleared everyone else, haven't we?"

"So, we're back to it being either Morris or Natalie, and the evidence against Morris is overwhelming."

"Unfortunately, I have to agree," Lilly said as they reached the top of the stairs. Suddenly the lights came on.

"Hurrah!" Chloe cried, taking the stairs two at a time.

"I'm just going to check my laptop to see if we've got internet connection," Lilly called after the speeding girl.

"Excellent!" she heard Robert say from the lounge. "The phone lines are working again. I'm going to call the police and get them up here as soon as possible."

Lilly gave a sigh of relief, glad this nightmare was finally over. The police would arrive as soon as the road was cleared, which Lilly expected would happen immediately once Robert told the police there was a murder victim currently in room four and the murderer staying in the house.

LILLY WENT TO her room and sat on the bed with her laptop, relieved to see the Wi-Fi was back on granting her access to the outside world. She wanted to check in with Stacey to see how things were with the shop and Earl. While she had left Stacey to run The Tea Emporium before, she'd never been out of contact for this long and hoped Stacey wasn't getting worried over her lack of communication.

Checking her email, she opened Stacey's first, pleased to see that everything was fine and running smoothly. She'd even attached a few pictures of Earl sleeping in her lap, snoozing in his favourite spot in the window and on Stacey's bed. He was obviously getting spoiled.

"Good," Lilly said, satisfied. She replied quickly, then opened up a search engine.

She was still having misgivings about the information they'd garnered and the resulting conclusions they had come to. If Morris had killed John, he had been out in that raging storm having just been involved in an accident, and his shoes and clothes would be wet and muddy. Would that old man have been able to make it from the car, back to the bed-and-breakfast where he killed a man, sneaked back out and then made it back to an abandoned clubhouse a great distance away in time to drink himself into a stupor, all without getting any signs of mud and water inside the house?

Admittedly Morris was an army man, but that sort of stealth and speed at his age was extremely unlikely. In fact, a man half his age would have had trouble achieving all that. It almost felt as though someone was attempting to frame him, and Lilly wanted to make sure she wasn't missing anything.

She spent a long time on her computer doing research, and she was thankful she'd taken the time and opportunity. She was right. The evidence they'd gathered didn't add up. She shook her head sadly. *I know who killed John*, she thought and closed her laptop before hurrying back downstairs to join the others.

Chapter Twelve

SHE ARRIVED JUST in time to greet the police with the rest of the household. Sam had taken charge, having announced to everyone that he was a private investigator, and was in the process of giving the police a blow by blow account of what had transpired in the previous few hours.

"We also eventually found Morris hiding out in the old clubhouse, a bit worse for wear due to a bottle of whiskey," Sam said, and Morris shifted uncomfortably in his seat.

"Morris isn't a killer," Robert said. "I just don't believe it. There's no indication he ever returned to the house after he left, and there would have been."

Once again Morris squirmed, but remained quiet.

"I agree," Joanne said, giving her husband a small smile. "It just doesn't make sense."

"Oh, so that's the way it's going to be, is it?" Natalie said, pointing a finger at them both. "You still think it was me. I'm telling you, I did not kill John."

"You were having an affair with him, Natalie," Sarah said angrily. "Maybe you were worried about getting caught?"

"Oh, of course, Sarah. I killed my lover to hide the fact I was sleeping with him, then left my underwear behind," Natalie said sarcastically. "That makes no sense at all. I ran from the room the moment I heard you knocking and hid at the far end of the passage until I was sure there was no one in the hall. I then left and came up straight behind you."

"Did you get the names of the police, Chloe?" Lilly whispered, coming to stand at her shoulder.

"Oh, hi. Yes, he's Officer Martins, and she's Detective Lacey. They're just trying to get the facts straight. I think the secret passage was a bit of a surprise."

"You sound as if you know them?"

"We all do, it's a small town."

"Okay," Lilly said. She decided to wait and keep the information she'd found on-line to herself for the moment. She didn't want to step on the toes of the police, and it would make more sense once the police knew everything else. There was also the fact of how devastating the news would be to all concerned. She was dreading it and could only hope the truth would be found before she had to speak.

"All right," Detective Lacey said. "Show me upstairs. And nobody leaves while I'm gone, understood? Officer Martins will remain here. We'll need to take a statement from each of you and I also have a crime scene team on the way."

"I'm not going anywhere, detective," Morris said quietly.

Robert led the detective to the next floor, followed closely by Sam, who volunteered to walk her through what had been uncovered so far.

Downstairs with everyone else, Lilly kept her eye on Morris, who was constantly fidgeting and wringing his hands. Unless they were being spoken to directly by the officer, the entire party kept quiet. Officer Martins was scribbling notes in his black book as the sequence of events was slowly unravelled. And he also announced that Detective Lacey would be speaking with everyone individually in the kitchen when she returned.

"This is going to be interesting," Chloe whispered to Lilly. "It's like an Agatha Christie book, isn't it? So, everyone will be interrogated one at a time by Detective Lacey? Do you think she'd let me help? I could be useful, don't you think? Maybe I should ask her."

"That's not a good idea, Chloe. Wait until it's your turn and help then."

Half an hour later, the detective was back with evidence bags dangling at her side. Lilly could see they contained the knife, the underwear, and the medal they'd found in the passage. She looked furious.

"Robert has just told me these items," she raised the bags. "Have been moved from their original positions. I'm sure you've all seen enough crime shows on television to know you never, ever tamper with a crime scene. Which one of you is responsible?"

Lilly sighed, and Detective Lacey's eyes immediately sought her out.

"I'm sorry, it was me. We were all trapped here and didn't know for how long. So, I looked around."

"I helped," Chloe suddenly said. Standing closer to Lilly in a show of alliance.

"And now your fingerprints are probably on everything."

"Oh, no, we were really careful," Chloe said.

Lacey held up the knife and the medal. "I assume these belong to one of our ex-servicemen?" she said, her gaze flitting from Jack to Morris and back. Jack smiled dreamily from his wheelchair, and Detective Lacey frowned. She pointed a finger at Morris. "I'll talk to you first."

MORRIS NERVOUSLY SHUFFLED after the detective and followed her into the kitchen. All eyes watched him in silence as he went. He looked like a man being sent to the gallows.

While Morris was being questioned, the crime scene technicians turned up. Officer Martins met them and after explaining where the murder had taken place and giving directions, they trooped upstairs armed with various cases and bags.

One by one, each of the staff and the family were called into the kitchen to be questioned by the detective. All of them cooperated fully, none of them wanting to make themselves seem guilty as they all appeared to have some sort of motive brewing underneath the surface.

J. NEW

Lilly was called in last, and like the others told Detective Lacey almost everything from the day she arrived. She also included her observations as an outsider, which while not strictly evidence, the detective was still interested in hearing. However, there was one pertinent discovery she kept to herself. Only time would tell whether she would need to share what she'd found.

Those couple of hours seemed to go by in a flash, and before they knew it, the detective was back in the lounge with them all, eyeing Morris with interest. It appeared to Lilly the woman had her suspicions already.

"Thank you all for your cooperation. We'll see what additional evidence the crime scene technicians find. They are an excellent team, so I'm certain we'll find what we need. I will of course require you all to submit to both DNA and fingerprint testing so we can eliminate those of you who are innocent."

Without warning, Morris jumped up.

"There's no need to do all that," he said. "I'm the one you want. I did it. I killed John. There's no need to put this family through any more, they are good people. I should have admitted it at the beginning rather than keeping quiet."

There was a collective gasp at the confession, and Sarah let out a shriek.

Lacey eyed him thoughtfully. "Let me confirm that. Are you confessing to the murder of John, Morris?"

"Yes, I am. I love this family, every one of them, and I've hated that man for years for how he treated them and the staff."

"All right," Lacey said. "Explain to me how you got in and out of here without leaving a trace and with no one seeing you."

Morris shrugged. "I was in the army. I know how to get in and out of a place without being seen. I know this place like the back of my hand, including the secret passage. That's my dagger and my medal. What more do you need?"

Lacey nodded. "In that case, Morris, I am..." she began, obviously about to arrest him.

"Wait," Lilly said quickly. She had hoped it wouldn't come to this, but she had to intervene.

"MORRIS, YOU CAN'T confess to something you didn't do, no matter what your reasons are. I know you didn't do it."

Morris glared at her. "Shut up. I told you I did it."

"What's the meaning of this, Miss Tweed?" Lacey asked.

"Lilly, what are you doing?" Joanne asked. "He just said he killed John and all the evidence says he did it."

"I'm so sorry, Joanne, Robert, Chloe. All of you. I've been wrestling with this ever since I found out. But Morris is protecting someone else. Morris, I can't in all good conscience let you take the blame for this. I know your confession comes from the heart, but I can't stand by and watch you get arrested for a murder you didn't commit. The person you're protecting should have the guts to stand up and tell the truth themselves. They are taking the coward's way out."

"Please, just shut up," Morris begged. "Let it go."

"Miss Tweed, unless you can explain what this is all about, I suggest you sit down," Detective Lacey said.

Then suddenly, Jack stood up. The shock in the room was palpable as everyone except Morris stared at the man, too bewildered to speak. Morris covered his face and collapsed into a nearby chair. "Dammit, Jack," he said softly.

Jack looked at Lilly. "I'm not a coward, Miss Tweed."

Robert and Sarah looked as though they would fall down at any moment, seeing their father upright and fully compos mentis. Lilly glanced at Chloe, who was staring at her granddad, bewildered and frightened as the truth suddenly dawned on her.

"Oh my god," Sam breathed, astounded. He too had thoroughly believed Morris had been the killer, and that Jack had been on his way to a fully vegetative state.

"Dad? Dad, sit down," Robert cried.

Jack shook his head. "I'm fine, son." Then he looked at the man who had been his best friend for more years than he could count. "It was the medal and dagger that helped you work it out, wasn't it, old friend?"

Morris nodded, tears streaming down his face. "Why did you get up, Jack? I was going to take the blame and would have done so happily. You saved my life once, it was my turn to save yours."

"I can't let you go to prison for something I did, Morris," Jack said. He turned to Lilly. "I understand how Morris worked out it was me. But what about you? How did you know?"

"Because of the Alzheimer's medicine that Chloe and I found. I've always had an interest in herbal medicine, particularly when it comes to tea. I recognised most of the list of ingredients on the bottle as being plant derivatives mixed with a sugar pill."

"Dad?" Sarah said.

Jack quickly glanced at his daughter, then looked away. "Go on," he said to Lilly.

"Your Alzheimer's isn't progressing as rapidly as you've led your family to believe. I realised what was happening when I saw the name of the doctor on the bottle. Your wife is a doctor, and she's the one who wrote the prescription. She's complicit too, isn't she, Jack?"

"Now wait just a minute, Lilly. What do you mean my mother's in on it? She's not even here," Robert said.

"No," Lilly said, feeling wretched at what she was having to do to her friends. "But she and Jack saw the perfect opportunity when his illness started to develop a plan to get rid of the man who was abusing their daughter."

"Oh no, dad," Sarah sobbed. "Tell me it's not true." The distress in her voice was obvious to everyone.

"I knew it wasn't Morris once we'd found the medal," Lilly continued softly. "Because he never received one. When I first arrived, Morris told me about you taking a bullet for him, Jack, saving his life. The medal was for your bravery. Once the power had returned, I made sure I was on the right lines by researching the recipients of that particular medal during the Falkland's conflict. There was no mention of Morris receiving a medal. But you were listed."

"That's right," Morris said quietly. "Jack's the hero."

"Is there anything else, Miss Tweed?" Detective Lacey asked.

Lilly nodded. "Yes, I'm afraid there is.

"Please, no more," Robert said, sinking onto a sofa, head in his hands. Joanne put her arm around her husband and laid her head on his shoulder.

"I'm sorry," Detective Lacey said. "But if there is more to this story, then I need to hear it. This is a murder investigation. Go on, Miss Tweed."

"There's no doubt Jack has Alzheimer's, but as you can see it's just not as advanced as was thought. Although it is getting worse and rapidly. It always struck me as strange that the murder weapon was left in the room. It was the one piece of pertinent evidence that would lead to the killer eventually, so why not remove it? It's certainly not a mistake a former service man would make."

"So, what do you think happened?" Detective Lacey asked.

"I believe Jack had some sort of episode, a seizure perhaps brought on by his illness and the stress of having just committed murder, where he forgot where he was for a moment and dropped the knife. When he came to, he heard all the commotion outside and realised he had to make his escape. In his haste, I think he accidentally kicked the knife under the bed. In the passage your medal probably dropped out of your pocket."

"Your lucky charm, dad," Sarah said.

There was a long pause as everyone let this revelation sink in. But Lilly wasn't finished.

"I'm sorry to have to say it, but I'm almost certain that Morris was in on it too."

"Don't you dare!" Jack warned, taking a step forward before Officer Martins took him by the arm, forcing him to remain where he was. "You've had your say, leave it at that."

"I can't, Jack. I'm truly sorry, but I need to tell the truth. You'd already put the plan into action by changing your medication and telling your family it was an experimental drug. I assume when all of this was over and someone else was in prison for the crime, your plan was to begin to improve, citing your alternative medicine as being responsible? Anyway, you decided the murder weapon would be your military knife, a purely arrogant choice as it happens. I put it down to some sort of misguided poetic justice. But Morris also had one, so to save him from getting the blame you warned him what you intended to do and made sure he was away from here when John died. Morris deliberately picked a fight with John, then left, but he got stuck. He may not have wielded the knife, but he certainly knew what was going to happen."

"You know," said Sam. "I always thought Morris's excuse that he couldn't find his way back here strange. He's worked here for years and knows the place as well as I do. It didn't make sense, especially when the clubhouse is not only further away but much more difficult to get to."

Lilly nodded. "Jack did everything he could to make sure himself, his wife and Morris couldn't possibly be arrested for the murder. His wife stayed behind, ostensibly for a well deserved spa break, but it was Morris that gave Robert and Sarah the idea in the first place. He staged the severity of his illness and he got Morris to promise to leave somehow. The military evidence pointed to them, but how could that be if one had diminished capacity and the other was absent? But then Natalie threw a spanner in the works by having an affair with John, and it made a mess of your plan. Am I right?"

Jack chuckled. "You think that wasn't part of the plan?" Once again the room stilled as all those present waited with bated breath to hear what Jack would say next. "I knew she and John were having an affair. You'd be amazed what people will say in front of you if they think you're a drooling idiot."

"Jack!" Natalie cried in shock. "You were trying to frame me for murder?"

"You and John hurt my daughter," he spat at her.

"Dad," Robert said, his voice shaking. "This isn't right. What you did. It's not right."

"I know, son. I know. But John will never hurt my daughter or anyone else again."

"Or you, Jack," Morris said. "I know he pushed you off that ladder."

Jack shook his head. "He didn't push me, Morris. I slipped, it was my own stupid fault."

"What? No, that can't be right. I saw the look he had on his face when you were falling, Jack. He was pleased."

"Yes, he was. Because he could have saved me, but he didn't. He might not have pushed me, Morris, but he didn't save me when he could. That's just as bad in my book. He was a blight on my family and a blight on this earth. He didn't deserve to live."

Chapter Thirteen

WHILE JACK WAS formally arrested and led away in handcuffs along with Morris, and Officer Martins made arrangements to pick up Jack's wife, Lilly slipped away to the kitchen. She felt the beginnings of a headache and wanted to make a cup of tea before it got any worse.

She was just sipping a freshly brewed cup of chamomile, which would also help with the stress and anxiety she was feeling, when Joanne came in.

"Lilly, I..."

"You want me to leave?"

Joanne nodded. "I'm sorry, Lilly, it's just with everything that's just happened, we, the family that is, need to be on our own."

"I understand, truly. I'm so sorry, Joanne, if it's any consolation I really was torn between keeping mouth shut and letting Morris take the blame, and telling what I knew. I wouldn't have deliberately hurt any of you for the world. You do know that, don't you?"

"I do, Lilly. But it doesn't make it any easier to stomach. Robert's just lost his parents having found out they murdered their son-in-law, and Chloe has lost her grandparents. Sarah's lost her husband and her parents. The family is broken, Lilly, and I don't know if it will ever heal. I... I'm sorry, Lilly, but it's for the best."

Joanne left and Lilly finished her tea, then went to pack. As she was loading her car, Chloe came out and gave her a tearful hug.

"Thank you for letting me be your Watson," she sniffed. "The police have found granddad's clothes, covered in blood hidden in the toilet cistern in his room. There was also some blood in the passage that we missed."

"Oh, Chloe. I can't tell you how sorry I am that it worked out the way it did."

"It wasn't your fault. I told dad and Joanne you had to tell the truth. Dad has always told me to tell the truth and take responsibility for my own actions. This is the same thing, isn't it? You had to do what was right."

Once again, Lilly was struck with how mature and sensible Chloe was.

"Yes. I couldn't have lived with myself if I'd kept quiet. I just wish things had worked out differently," she explained, as tears welled in her own eyes.

Chloe nodded. "I know. I hope I get to see you again, Lilly. Maybe you could email me sometimes?"

Lilly promised she would, then watched as the girl ran back to the house, wiping tears on her sleeve as she went.

Tiffin & Tragedy

The drive back to Plumpton Mallet was long and silent. What had started as a happy celebration for two of her friends had ended in a tragedy so serious she didn't know if her friendship with Robert and Joanne would survive. It upset her deeply, and her mind was caught in a loop, replaying the sequence of events over and over. But she still came to the same conclusion. She couldn't have remained silent and let a man get away with murder. No matter who he was.

Two hours into her journey home, the phone rang. She answered automatically via Blue-tooth without checking who the caller was.

"Lilly, it's Joanne. Listen, I just want you to know we don't blame you in any way for what happened. I know you feel somewhat responsible, Chloe told us, but you shouldn't, Lilly. Jack made his choices and he'll have to live with them. Unfortunately, we'll also have to live with his actions. But Robert and I wanted you to know we both feel awful for how we let you leave. We're all reeling and distraught, but we should have behaved better."

"It doesn't matter, Joanne, honestly," Lilly said, full of relief that her friend was still speaking to her. "How are Robert and Sarah?"

"They've both suffered through every emotion possible since you left. Robert's just gone out with Walter to clear the remains of the fallen trees. The police arranged for a partial clearance so they could get through, but there's still a lot to do. I think doing something physical will help him. Sarah, as you can imagine, is blaming herself. If she hadn't married John, or if she'd had the strength to leave him, then it would never have come to this. That's what she's saying. But there's also a part of her that's relieved John is gone. I think when the dust settles I'll suggest she find a therapist to talk to."

"Yes, that's a good idea. What about Natalie?"

"She packed and left for good fifteen minutes ago. I'll give her a positive reference. She was excellent at her job after all and was very nearly made a scapegoat in Jack's scheme, but we can't employ her after what happened."

"No, of course not. Joanne, I know you all have a long road ahead of you and it will be difficult. If there's anything I can do to help you, will let me know, won't you?"

"Yes, I will. Thanks, Lilly. I've got to go and make a phone call now. Detective Lacey gave me the details of a specialist cleaning company for room four now they've all left. I was going to tackle it myself but I just can't bring myself to even go in there. What does it say about our society that there's a need for specialist companies who clean up crime scenes? Anyway, I'll be in touch. Take care, Lilly."

"You too, Joanne."

LILLY HAD SENT a quick text to Stacey informing her she was on her way home, but it would be late so she wouldn't be in the shop until the following morning, if she wouldn't mind looking after Earl for one more night. As expected, Stacey was more than happy to look after the cat.

The next day she was at The Tea Emporium, bright and early, but Stacey had still beaten her to it and was already setting everything up in readiness for opening.

When she entered, Earl jumped out of his usual spot in the window and came to greet her, purring loudly and weaving through her legs. She bent to pick him up. "I missed you too, Earl."

"Lilly, you're back," Stacey called, exiting the store room.

"I am. How were things while I was gone?"

"Really busy, but nothing I couldn't handle. Everyone asked where you were and when I told them, they all said you deserved a break. So, how was the party? Did you have a good time? I saw you had a massive storm down there. I hope it didn't ruin the celebrations?"

Lilly sighed. "Actually, it all started well then went horribly wrong," she said. And proceeded to tell Stacey all that had happened.

"Oh, Lilly, that's just awful. I'm so sorry. But I believe you did the right thing. What will happen to them?"

Lilly shook her head. "I don't know, Stacey. Jack may plead some sort of mental health breakdown due to his illness. I suppose it depends on how good his solicitor is. He may live out the rest of his days in an institution rather than prison, although there'll come a time when his memory will fail and he won't remember any of it, anyway. Regarding his wife and Morris, I don't know. It had been planned for a while so would be classed as premeditated, but there were extenuating circumstances because of John's abuse of Sarah and the fact he didn't save Jack from having the accident when he could have. There are plenty of witnesses to what a destructive and dangerous person John was. Morris was prepared to take the fall for a man who saved his life. It's a minefield which a good legal team will have to wade through. I suppose we'll have to wait and see what happens."

"Well, after all you've been through, I think a cup of tea is in order. The new lavender blend arrived yesterday, good for helping anxiety and calming you down. What do you say?"

"Make it a large one please, Stacey."

With the tea drunk and the shop ready to open, Stacey took a slip of paper from the message pile. "I have an interesting request for you. A couple came in, newly engaged and would like a fully vintage afternoon tea style wedding. They would like you to do it."

"Really? A wedding?" Lilly said, taking the note from Stacey. "That's a lot bigger than the small book club event I did at Mrs Davenport's."

"I know, right?" Stacey said excitedly. "I told you events were the thing. Mrs Davenport and Lady Defoe have been raving about your teas and tea parties. I guess word must have spread."

"A wedding would be interesting to do, actually. It sounds like fun, not to mention lucrative. But it would be a huge amount of work for just the two of us."

"Yeah, I know. They also want the catering doing."

"I only do teas, and special cocktails if asked which I would do for a wedding, but not food."

"I know, but I had an idea about that. What if we asked the owner of one of the local cafes to do that side of things? You know, like a joint venture. I'm sure one of them would be really interested in doing this type of event. You never know it could lead to lots more bookings."

"Hmm... you know, that's actually a really good idea, Stacey. Well done. I'll have a look round and send out some feelers later," Lilly said with a huge grin. "But for now, let's get this show on the road and open the shop. I've missed this place, Stacey. It's very good to be home."

If you enjoyed *Tiffin & Tragedy*, the third book in the Tea & Sympathy series, please leave a review on Amazon. It really does help other readers find the books.

About the Author

J. New is the author of *THE YELLOW COTTAGE VINTAGE MYSTERIES,* traditional English whodunits with a twist, set in the 1930's. Known for their clever humour as well as the interesting slant on the traditional murder mystery, they have all achieved Bestseller status on Amazon.

J. New also writes two contemporary cozy crime series:

THE TEA & SYMPATHY series featuring Lilly Tweed, former newspaper Agony Aunt now purveyor of fine teas at The Tea Emporium in the small English market town of Plumpton Mallet. Along with a regular cast of characters, including Earl Grey the shop cat.

THE FINCH & FISCHER series featuring mobile librarian Penny Finch and her rescue dog Fischer. Follow them as they dig up clues and sniff out red herrings in the six villages and hamlets that make up Hampsworthy Downs.

Jacquie was born in West Yorkshire, England. She studied art and design and after qualifying began work as an interior designer, moving onto fine art restoration and animal portraiture before making the decision to pursue her lifelong ambition to write. She now writes full time and lives with her partner of twenty-two years, two dogs and five cats, all of whom she rescued.

If you would like to be kept up to date with new releases from J. New, you can sign up to her *Reader's Group* on her website www.jnewwrites.com You will also receive a link to download the free e-book, *The Yellow Cottage Mystery*, the short-story prequel to The Yellow Cottage Vintage Mystery series.

Printed in Great Britain
by Amazon